WOLF RETREAT

N GRAY

BOOKS

By N Gray

Shifter Days, Vampire Nights & Demons in Between

Twisted

Lady Hawk and Her Mountain Man

Hidden Shifter

Wolf

Wolf Retreat

Night Hunter

The Fixer

Kai

Lee

Flynn

Jude

Scout Thorne

The Secret Tomb

Murder of Crows

Blaire Thorne

Ulysses Exposed

Voodoo Priest

Butterflies and Hurricanes

Salvation

Underworld Legacy

The Dana Mulder Suspense Thriller Series

Deadly Pattern

Devil Mountain

Chasing Evil

Nightcrawler

Horror

What's for Dinner

Creature Features

Monster Features

Thrillers

Lady Killer

More from N Gray

writing as Natalie Michaels

Steve Campbell Psychological Suspense Thrillers

The Last Girl

The Bone Forest

The White Dahlia

I See You

Death in the City

More from N Gray

writing as SD Syns

The Diaries

Red Lace Diaries

www.ngraybooks.com

Vinci Books

vinci-books.com

Published by Vinci Books Ltd in 2026

1

The publisher and the author have made every effort to obtain permissions
for any third party material used in this book and to comply with copyright
law. Any queries in this respect should be brought to the attention of the
publisher and any omissions will be corrected in future editions.
A CIP catalogue record for this book is available from the British Library.
Paperback ISBN: 9781036702212
The EU GPSR authorised representative is Logos Europe, 9 rue Nicolas
Poussion, 17000 La Rochelle, France contact@logoseurope.eu

Chapter One

CARMEN

I packed my bag with more than enough clothing to last two weeks instead of the required five days. Gina would arrive soon, and then we'd be off for a retreat. The thought of taking a few days off sounded great, but we wouldn't be taking it easy, we had work to do.

We needed to find a new alpha to lead our pack before the rogue pack captured and separated the remaining wolves. The threats we'd received since they'd killed John, our alpha, were insurmountable. What set us all on edge? They wanted our females.

The knuckles rapping on my front door pulled me from my thoughts. I unlocked and opened my front door to greet Gina, who wore an expression matching my own; disbelief, panic, with a hint of petrified.

"Are you ready?" She asked carefully and stepped inside.

"As ready as I'll ever be. Do you know if they have hairdryers? You know I need to tame this mane of mine." I didn't feel like discussing the elephant in the room and would rather focus on mundane topics as I combed my fingers through my freshly blowdried hair.

My question brought a thin smile to her face and her eyes twinkled before reverting to that shocked state.

"They even have beds, lights, and food. Can you imagine?" She gasped. "And we don't have to gather our own meals."

I slapped her shoulder. "Come in, Miss Sarcasm. Let me grab my stuff so we can get going." I left Gina in the kitchen while I went to my bedroom.

Paper being unwrapped echoed in my quaint apartment, followed by loud chewing, then a pop.

"I'm amazed your jaw isn't square from chewing all day every day," I said as I slung the strap of my duffle bag over my shoulder.

"You're so funny," she said as she chewed open-mouthed.

I narrowed my eyes. "You look like a cow, at least close your mouth. How are you going to find anyone chewing like that?" The moment the words left my mouth, I regretted it and shook my head. "I'm sorry." I cautiously approached her. She batted my hand away, spit her bubble gum in my sink, and walked across the open-plan kitchen/lounge area toward the front door.

"You're right," she said sadly. "It's a habit I need to correct." Her voice sounded small and hurt, and my chest ached.

"I'm sorry, I really am. I shouldn't have said that." I exhaled a shaky breath.

Gina rocked the plain-Jane-look with a striking difference; her honey-colored hair glittered. It looked like silver flecks shimmered in her hair depending on how the sunlight caught it. Her father was a purebred wolf while

2

her mother was fae. Their relationship was volatile as one imagined, yet they made it work. While they moved North with their pack, Gina had settled with me, her wolf-bestie, in my hometown Krystal Creek and joined our tiny wolf pack.

"Come, let's start over." I forced a smile even though it wavered at the sides. I did not feel brave and doubted Gina did too.

Gina removed the pack of gum from her pocket and threw it on my coffee table with a loud thud. "I quit," she announced. "From today on, no more gum. It will be hard, but I have to. I know what I look like chewing," she said, her smile genuine, and it reached her hazel-colored eyes.

I was so proud of her, she'd come so far. It was easy for Gina to become hooked on whichever substance was available, whether it was cigarettes, alcohol, or narcotics. Being a were-wolf meant she had to consume copious amounts before she felt anything, and then she'd double that amount and then some.

She'd progressed through all the substances and gave them up, and was now chewing bubblegum like her life depended on it. In some ways it was, she was afraid she'd relapse and start drinking again. With everything that was going on, perhaps having a shot of alcohol now and again would help. But I didn't want to mess with her sobriety. Come to think of it. I didn't think it was a good idea for her to stop chewing bubblegum.

"Are you sure? You might need it?" I picked up the pack of gum and slipped it in my pocket while Gina remained silent. "How about we do this, I'll keep the pack and if you feel you need it, I'll give you one. Then you spit it out once you've had your fix."

She grinned and gave a curt nod. "Fine, now let's go. I

3

think the moment we're on the road these butterflies in my stomach will go away," she groaned, rubbing her tummy.

I threw my duffel bag into the back seat of her car beside her bag and climbed into the passenger seat. Gina pressed the Start button and her Audi roared to life. She did well for herself and contributed toward our pack. Where she thrived in the corporate world, hiding her true wolf-self, I preferred working in solitude as a freelance graphic designer from the comfort of my home. I made enough to get by, with a small savings for rainy days, but that was it. I didn't need a car since everything I needed was here. Our pack was so small everyone lived together in one large apartment building. If I needed to go anywhere, I caught a ride with Gina. I didn't know what I'd do without her. She's my bestie and we'd come a long way since we were young.

I thought of John and how he had brought everybody under one roof to protect us, like a father would. Although he was gone, we still had each other.

But now... now we had nobody powerful enough within our pack to protect us.

"I didn't know what music you felt like listening to, so I just downloaded a bunch of oldies," Gina said, bringing me out of my reverie. "Our destination is two hours away toward those mountains." She pointed at the ominous mountain range surrounding our small town. "There should be enough music to last us the trip."

If we traveled West, we'd hit Sterling Meadow, another town but much bigger than Krystal Creek and with a much larger Wolf Pack. They would be our last hope if we didn't succeed in the next five days. A retreat where alphas from all over the country convened in one location, spent time with females up for the challenge, and hopefully half walked away with their fated mate. Whether Gina and I would find our alpha, we could only pray.

We continued our journey in silence. The radio played her music, but I doubted she heard any of it. I barely caught the words of any songs as I stared out the window, watching nature blur past us as we wound our way through the mountainous road.

The thought of our small pack being ripped apart left a hollow feeling in my stomach. I didn't want to move away, Krystal Creek had been my home since I was a teenager. And John had been like a father to me when my own parents had abandoned me. The possibility of leaving hung around my neck like a noose. If I failed the rope would tighten its hold on me.

Our pack was small compared to others; we were thirty wolves, but only ten were male. But none old or dominant enough to be our alpha. Of the twenty females, most were under the age of eighteen.

When the rogue wolf pack attacked our clubhouse and killed John, they gave us ten days to replace him and fight JT, their alpha. We couldn't allow this rogue pack to win again. They had indicated they wanted our girls. They needed our females to continue their bloodlines. We would have to endure another fight to the death and if they won, again, we had to give up our rights and agree to join their pack.

Since Gina and I were the oldest, we had offered to attend this retreat to save our pack. Attending this retreat was important. A matter of life or death. And we had to make it work.

Chapter Two

SHAWN

My truck was packed and ready to go, but I couldn't do it. With much to do for the Wolf Pack before I left, I didn't think I'd make the retreat in time. The Were-Animal Alliance, WAA, needed my help regarding a rogue pack of wolves destroying smaller packs. I needed to figure out what to do since this smaller pack had approached us for help. I was thinking of sending one of my strongest to them, but I worried the rogue pack would slaughter him. We required a strategy where everybody walked away happy. Nobody wanted a war.

Jason entered my office with a knowing look. "You should've left already," he stated.

"I know, but there are things I need to do before I go."

"You're supposed to tell me what needs to be done, and I'll do it. That's why I'm your second," he grumbled, although his eyes held humor.

I exhaled, glanced down at my desk with papers everywhere and knew he was right. I was stalling. It had been over three years since I'd started my search for a mate. And nothing. I'd even put a call out for prospective females from many towns and dated three per day for a month, searching for the right one. None came close to stirring my beast. *Not one!* I must've met about three thousand, kissed half, and slept with a few and nothing. My dark beast didn't want any of them.

"You're right," I said, setting down my pen. "There are things that need completing for the WAA. These are for the clubhouse. This pile is for the new initiatives—"

"I get it, Shawn, you can go. I know what to do, I've been helping you for months." He arched an eyebrow.

I pushed back my chair and slowly stood up. "Alright," I said with a nod. "I need to see if she's there."

"Yes."

"Our pack will become stronger when that happens."

"Yep."

"You will call me if there's trouble."

"Absolutely."

"You're very agreeable today."

"That I am," he grinned.

"You just want me out."

Jason laughed. "I want you to relax and see if you can find your mate. Your pack will still be here for you if you don't. You know I won't challenge you and although I'm not *the* alpha, I'm an alpha who would do everything for *our* pack. And through my bonding, I've shared my power with us. It will have to be enough until you find her."

Jason had recently found his fated mate and bonded. The sudden surge of power we all had felt was like an electric bolt coursing through our veins and fueling our land. Everywhere we walked, their power continued to hum around us. We all felt stronger, we healed even quicker, and it tied us closer to each other.

I should've been the one with the shared power.

Jason had every right to challenge me. But he didn't want to. He was content being my second. But if anyone challenged me, the possibility of them killing me was greater because I hadn't mated yet. I needed that extra boost of power in order to protect my family, and my pack.

"I know. And thank you."

We shook hands. He patted my shoulder and wore a sympathetic expression. I knew the pack were concerned about whether my mate was even alive yet. I'd been leader of this pack for many years and although I was strong enough to have lasted this long, the thought of continuing without a mate was wearing me down.

I grabbed my cellphone, truck keys and jacket, and headed toward my vehicle without saying another word. If I didn't find my mate on this retreat, I'd go on the next one, and the next one.

A friend of mine had suggested this company. They serviced high power alphas who struggled to find their mates. It was by invitation only, and my friend got me on their VIP list. While any female, human or were-wolf, was welcome to attend once screened.

There were ten alphas from all over the country attending the five-day retreat. Each pack leader in a similar situation to me, I could only hope that all that testosterone won't cost us dearly.

The two-hour drive was scenic; the winding road through the mountains helped ease my busy mind. If I wanted to meet anyone, I needed to chill. Nobody wanted an uptight partner.

I finally arrived at the venue shortly after lunch. The monstrous building reminded me of the hotel from *The Shining*. I hoped there were no ghosts.

A man greeted me as I pulled up to the entrance. He smelled like a wolf and something else I couldn't put my finger on. He called over a valet who grabbed my bags while another one took the keys for my truck. They moved swiftly and efficiently, and so far impressed me. I guessed for the price tag to be here; they had to treat us like kings.

"My name is Olson and I'm the day manager. You must be Shawn, alpha of the Wolf Pack in Sterling Meadow," he said, shaking my hand.

"Yes," I said with furrowed brows and wiped my hand on my jeans. I had no idea how Olson knew me, and when I shook his hand, a strange power zapped up my arm, leaving pins and needles in its wake.

He must've understood my silent question, for he added. "They require us to study all applicants once we receive your paperwork and you're accepted. And please accept my apologies for the power, I'm part wolf, part fae with an electric current constantly running through me. But don't worry, you're perfectly safe. My power is under control. I only use it against trespassers." Olson combed his fingers through his shoulder length black hair with light blue streaks. Tiny blue sparks shot from his fingers to the strands of hair. His actions left me guarded as I watched him walk toward the entrance before realizing he wanted me to follow him.

Once I caught up to him, we entered the luxurious hotel. The cool air blasted against my hot skin and Olson removed his sunglasses, revealing lavender eyes. I noted his pointy ears and wondered what color his wolf was since his hair was so dark.

"I'm a blue were-wolf," he said with smiling eyes.

"Blue wolf? Like the color?"

"Yes, the color blue."

"And you read minds?"

"I pick up on mannerisms, slight gestures, that kind of thing. Plus, I get asked that question all the time when they find out I'm fae and I'm a blue were-wolf," he smiled.

"Are you the only blue wolf here?" I thought blue were-wolves were a myth, yet one stood before me. Perhaps I should ask him for an autograph.

"No, there are many of us living in the surrounding area." He didn't offer any additional information nor did I push. It made me wonder why they weren't more visible and the reason he was so guarded.

In the foyer was no check-in counter, only chairs and tables with a bar area to one side. The smell of roast beef wafted in the air, making me salivate.

"You're welcome to use any part of this room. You may drink anything at anytime, but we would like to request that you don't go overboard. It's a strange request I know, but we've had to escort alphas out because they overindulged with crass behavior." We continued walking as he gave me the grand tour. "Each alpha has their own suite. Inside each suite is a king sized bed, kitchenette and small living area. You're welcome to hunt from the vast land available to you, or order from room service. Whichever is convenient." We stopped by a set of doors, which he opened. "The Ballroom is where we host the dinners. We require each alpha to attend and sample the females."

"What do you mean by sample?"

"Nothing sinister, I assure you, and we abuse none of the females. Just think of it as a sushi bar, but instead of the sushi moving around you, it's the females. None are to be touched. It's purely to see whether any female calls out to an alpha."

That made sense, but strange to have women moving around on a moving walkway. The stage before me looked like walkways seen at airports, shaped like a long horseshoe. In the center of the horseshoe shape were chairs spaced apart.

"Does that happen tonight?"

"Yes, once all the females arrive. Until then you are welcome to engage with those here or you can lounge in your room." He produced a set of keys, handing them to me. "Or you can use the health gym, the indoor pool on the top floor, or the one outside. You can basically go anywhere, except this door." Olson pointed to a set of doors behind me.

"What's there?"

Olson smirked as if every alpha asked that question. "That's where the females sleep."

A nervousness swept over me, one I hadn't considered before, and needed an answer. "Are these females willing, Olson?"

Olson's eyebrows shot up as if I slapped him. "What? Absolutely, Shawn. We do not threaten or harm any female, nor do we force them to be here. My gods," he gasped, clutching his chest as his face blossomed into a shade redder. "We are a professional body and everything we do is above board. If you still have concerns, I can take you to our Managing Director." He thumbed behind him. I peered over his left shoulder at the name plaque near another door.

"It's okay, but I feel comfortable knowing they did not traffic these women."

Olson sucked in deep breaths. I thought he was going to hyperventilate. It was only after five minutes he calmed down and finally added. "I take it you didn't read the documents we sent over?"

"Uh," I stammered. He caught me there, I hadn't had the time to read the hundred page document.

Olson smiled knowingly, no longer as flustered. "It's okay, there's another information pack in your room. In there you'll find the details. But I'll go over it to put your mind at ease. Alpha's need to be referred to us by others who've been here. We do extensive background checks into each and if we're content, we send invites. This is an elite club and although we've had our fair share of troublemakers, it remains prestigious. The females are human or were-wolves themselves and come voluntarily. They understand what this event is and are bound by confidentiality. We'll take legal action against anyone who utters a word outside this club about what we do or how we do it. The reason is due to competition."

I suspected it was because of the money involved, because the price tag wasn't cheap.

"The females don't pay," Olson continued. "That is why the alpha's costs are so high. Each female receives the same background check and screening prior to acceptance, and they may leave at any time. They do not have to stay the five days and if they have complaints against any alpha, we will investigate." Olson's cheeks were back to their healthy brown shade and his eyes a lilac color. "Are you satisfied with my answer?" He asked straight-faced.

"Yes, thank you. Would you mind showing me my room?"

"May I suggest you walk around," — with his index finger he circled the air beside his head, — "look at the amenities and say '*hi*' to your fellow alphas. I would like to remind you it is not a competition. Your fated mate will

12

become yours, and yours alone. Therefore, we do not allow any fighting among the alphas. If that happens, we ban you for life." He arched an eyebrow for effect.

"Thanks, I'll go this way." I pointed to my right.

"Very well, sir. Dinner in the Ballroom is at six and please wear the proper attire." Olson made a sharp right turn as if he was in the army and marched to the front door.

Jeez, he was high-strung and desperately needed to get laid himself, but I understood his concerns. But at the same time, I needed my questions addressed. The last thing I wanted was a room full of abused women. I'd call my were-brothers from home and take the lot out. We didn't condone that type of behavior. No female should be forced into anything.

"He needs to remove that stick from his ass," a man said behind me.

I turned around and craned my neck up. "Christ, you're huge." The mountain of a man was about eight feet tall with broad shoulders and biceps the size of my muscular thighs. The strongly built man not only radiated power but wore an expression informing me he was a softie. A gentle giant who could crush you if needed.

"The name's Nick," he said, holding out a large hand.

"I can see why you're here," I said, shaking his hand. For a change it wasn't a pissing contest, and he didn't break my hand, nor did he have sweaty palms. "Shawn from Sterling Meadow."

"Yeah, I tend to scare the ladies away and the ones who approach me shouldn't be touched with a ten-foot pole," he chuckled. The low rumbling sound echoed in the hallway. "If you want a drink, grab one where we're sitting." Nick thumbed behind him where the umbrellas were up and someone was swimming.

"I first want to walk around the place."

"Come, it's better if you walk with someone." Nick slapped my shoulder and turned me around to follow him.

I followed Nick and rubbed the shoulder he'd slapped. I was big but Nick was huge; powerfully built. I'd never want to be on the receiving end of his fists.

The first floor was where the alphas slept. On the second floor was the gym and sauna, and the third floor was the heated indoor pool and outdoor patio.

They spared no expense. Every table strategically placed with fresh flowers and adorned on the walls were paintings and light fixtures I'd seen in luxury magazines. Even the air smelled clean, with a hint of freshness I couldn't decipher.

We traversed down a set of stairs near the exit by the pool. Lounging near the pool and bar area were three other men. Usually, when more than three unknown alpha males occupied the same space, there was a certain amount of testosterone needed to show dominance. But with these guys, I sensed nothing other than their scent—*wolf*. We weren't here to fight to the death. We were here for the same thing; searching for our fated mate and until now we had failed in finding her. We all needed help.

As I entered the outdoor pool area with the giant behind me, power from the males spiked in a fight-or-flight instinct, then settled down again. Regardless of the circumstance, we all had instincts and whether there was any danger. But there were none at the moment.

Nick introduced me. By the time introductions were over, I'd already forgotten their names. I was great with faces, but not with names. I remembered the blond was from Texas, the dark-skinned alpha from New Orleans, and the red-head from Nashville. Nick was from Atlantis.

"The best are those with green eyes," Nashville said with a sly smirk. "Imagine the pups we'll have." His green eyes glistened in the light. "I've waited so long. I have to find her here… no matter what."

"It's not like you can force the female to bond," Nick said, arching an eyebrow.

"Of course not. That would be cruel."

"I'll have another drink," Texas said, standing up offering the others if they wanted.

After Texas had his drink the barman poured me a neat whiskey which I downed and then another one. I sat in an available chair and listened to their conversation. I'd contribute to the conversation every now and then but I mostly just listened.

It was nice to sit and do nothing but drink and listen. We did that at the clubhouse at full moon, but I was always in work-mode. I'd listen to my wolves, but in the back of my mind thoughts about what I had to do always came to the surface and I never switched off—even at night. I rarely slept over four or five hours a night, even though I trained daily and went to bed exhausted.

Sitting among these men, where I was completely out of my comfort zone, was refreshing.

The two hours flew by and during that time the remaining alphas had joined us. By five o'clock the barman chased us away, reminding us we needed to get ready for dinner at six.

I followed the men to the first floor and found room nine at the end of the hall. Nick was in room ten and offered to knock on my door at 5:55pm.

My suite had all the luxuries required for an executive. I

grabbed my duffle bag off the floor, set it on the bed, and removed my suit. Luckily there were hardly any wrinkles in the material and hung it up.

My thoughts crashed back to Sterling Meadow, and I knew I had to find out what was going on back home or I'd become miserable. I called Jason and he told me to stop calling and would phone if anything happened. I took the hint, ended the call and showered.

Chapter Three

CARMEN

Gina and I shared a room with twin beds. It had a tiny kitchenette and bathroom with a shower. The room was small but tastefully decorated and I didn't feel cramped.

"There's no hairdryer," Gina said as she exited the bathroom, zipping up her jeans.

"What?" I basically yelled and darted for the bathroom to check.

"Just kidding!" She sang.

"Brat!" I slapped her shoulder as I pushed past her and entered the bathroom. "Wow, it's actually nice," I said, opening drawers beneath the basin to see what they offered. The first drawer was a selection of creams, cotton wool, perfumes and makeup. In the second drawer they had a hairdryer and curling iron. On the basin stood two different flavored toothpastes and extra toothbrushes. The mirror opened with a thumb to the corner. Inside held a selection of pain medication and everything found in a first-aid kit.

"They have everything in here and more."

"Isn't it lovely? I almost forgot why we were here," Gina

said, poking her head around the doorjamb. "I've a good feeling about this. We have to be positive, don't we?" Her eyes glistened in the radiant light.

"I want to be positive. I really do. But I'm afraid the moment I do, something terrible is going to go wrong."

"I understand, I get that too. But... I dunno," she shrugged, "the moment we entered those enormous gates and drove up that long driveway, I actually felt good about it. I didn't get that sinking feeling the world was about to end, or we're going to become someone's meal. I just know it's going to be fun." She disappeared before I could answer, then popped back into the bathroom. "And we're going to find our alpha." And she disappeared again.

"I hope so," I called after her. "Even if its only you who finds your forever mate, then it was worth coming here," I said, trying my best to sound happy.

In some packs, females found their mate fairly early in their life. For the lucky ones, they found them the night of their first shift at eighteen. Usually from the ages of twenty till about thirty-five, almost all females would be with their partner. I was pushing forty-one and was pretty sure most considered me an old maid. Our alpha never forced me to find my mate, nor did he kick me out of our pack for not having one. I didn't look forty and was extremely fit, so it never really bothered me until five minutes ago.

Gina was twenty-nine. She thought she had found her mate, but he ended up ditching her on their second date. This happened a couple of months ago and she still didn't know why.

Someone knocked softly on our door, and I headed to see who it was.

"Evening ladies, I'm Valerie, the night manager." Valerie was a goddess in stilettos. She was almost six feet tall, skinny, with large breasts and wore an extravagant evening gown.

Oh gods, we were so underdressed.

Valerie caught sight of my expression and smiled. "You must be Carmen," — she pointed at me, — "and you are Gina." We nodded in unison. "May I come in for a moment?"

"Sure," Gina said, opening the door wider for her to enter.

"I welcome all guests personally. Not only the alphas but the women too," she smiled sweetly. Her lips the perfect shade of red to match her gown and shoes. "Gina, based on your answers we have paired you with the alpha from New Orleans during dinner. The seating arrangements aren't permanent, if you find you're attracted to someone else you can let me know and we will move you. Carmen, you are our oldest female at the retreat. Naturally we welcome all ages between twenty and fifty, and all races. Based on your answers, we've partnered you with the alpha from Nashville. As I've said, everything may change after your initial intro-duction to the alphas."

Valerie continued explaining what we had to do before dinner even started and my stomach dropped to my shoes. I didn't like the idea of standing on a moving walkway parading in front of the alphas like livestock. I felt blood drain from my body by the time Valerie ended her instruc-tions. She unlocked the tiny closet revealing four evening dresses, each tailored specific to our bodies. It impressed me, but it didn't feel right.

When I closed the door after Valerie left, I needed a break and fresh air. But we were told to stay put until 6 pm.

"I think I'm going to throw up." I darted past Gina and dry heaved into the toilet bowl. A shudder ran through me as I thought about lining up for the alphas. It wasn't so much the meeting part that left me on edge, but being displayed. I washed my face and brushed my teeth.

"What's wrong?"

"Didn't you hear what she told us to do? Doesn't it bother you?"

"No, why would it?"

"We have to parade for these men—"

"How else are they supposed to see us, Carmen? They aren't auctioning us off to the highest bidder. We aren't naked on stage and bending over. We're here to find our mate and this must happen."

"But its demeaning and derogatory."

Gina cocked out her hip and stared at me like I sprouted a third head. "Where's this coming from? You're not a feminist."

"No, I'm not standing near buildings shouting for women's rights, but I get strange feelings that might put me on edge. Like now."

"It's going to be fine."

"I hope so." I sat on my bed, opting to lie down instead. We had over an hour to get ready and I needed my head cleared. Perhaps it was because I was the oldest that these types of things left a strange taste in my mouth. Or I was more of a prude than I wanted to admit. But… I didn't know what it was. I felt strange and regretted coming here.

"I'm done!" Gina called, waking me. She stood on her side of the bedroom, fixing herself a drink. "Do you want one?" She held up her glass of wine.

"Are you sure you should drink that?" Gina had a habit

of consuming certain substances and even though she was a wolf and it affected us differently, it still affected her.

"I'm fine. I promise. Is not excessive drinking like I used to do. Besides, it's only a light wine." She held up the bottle as she read the alcohol content. "And I'm not hitting the heavy stuff."

"Promise?"

"Promise," she smiled. "I'm fine."

"Yeah, I'll have one," I said, staring at her carefully. Not that a glass of wine would affect me much, but I needed *something*. I still felt on edge. "I'm going to shower quickly."

"You have half an hour," she yelled as she clinked glasses and giggled.

"How many have you had?" I asked as I stripped naked.

"A bottle." She hiccuped and handed me my glass of wine. "I'm fine and besides, I'm nervous and drank a bit too quickly that's all."

Thank heavens we needed more than a bottle of wine to affect us since our metabolisms were so fast, but still. I arched an eyebrow at her as I sipped. The wine tasted like it came from the fruits of the gods.

"This is delicious."

"Apparently they spare no expense for the females." Gina emphasized the word *females* like it was a swearword.

"What's wrong?"

"Nothing… It's just, I've been thinking about what you said and maybe you're right. But we still need to do it. They said we could leave any time we wanted to, but we can't. Not now. We're running out of time, Carmen," she said, eyes glistening. "If this doesn't work, we need to beg the alpha from Sterling Meadow to help us fight the rogue's."

I nodded as I sipped, still standing naked but not embarrassed. We stood naked before each other all the time without it being sexual.

"Let me shower quickly and then we can chat some more. But you are right," I said, setting my glass on the counter and opened the hot water.

I showered quickly, dried my body then blow dried my hair. The gowns they'd left us were stunning. Both of mine were strapless, meaning I'd have to go braless. It wasn't ideal, but at least the dresses had an internal corset lifting my breasts, and giving me wonderful cleavage.

"Holy smokes, you look hot." Gina gawked at me from where she stood near the mirror. "If anyone knew your age, they would forget it the moment they saw you in that dress."

"Thanks," I said, although I groaned inwardly. I'd just forgotten the concern I had regarding my age, and now she brought it up again. I stood behind her while she applied makeup and I fixed the green gown to neaten the petticoat. I hadn't even added makeup yet and my green eyes popped, making them look a shade lighter than they usually were.

"With your black hair and green eyes that dress really makes you stand out, Carmen," Gina said, her mouth hanging open like she was a Venus flytrap.

"Thank you. You look ravishing yourself."

She wore the purple gown that accentuated her curvy figure and brought out the silver in her hair. She smiled sadly, then continued applying makeup.

"I guess if we go home empty-handed you could always try?" She said while applying eyeliner like a pro.

I stared wide eyed at her. "What do you mean?"

"I know we haven't spoken about it. Maybe you could fight the rogue."

I blinked at Gina. My words caught in my throat. I'd

thought about leading but never dreamed the others might want me to head the pack. I hadn't considered it seriously.

"I don't know. JT would kill me quickly," I said, giving her a deadpan stare. JT had killed our alpha leader within seconds of the fight starting. My body felt numb as thoughts bounced around in my mind. I honestly didn't know if I could beat JT and if I did, would I be accepted as the alpha? I wasn't sure I wanted it, anyway.

"Everybody already looks up to you," she said. "It's just natural for me to think that you could lead us. Besides, you already do so much for us anyway. And now that John's gone, you have his power too," she said carefully, avoiding my eyes.

Our pack ancestors had deemed me worthy of the power of those fallen. I didn't know what it meant, and it scared me. I knew of a handful of females powerful enough to lead their own packs, but I wasn't like them.

"It's just a thought. Think nothing of it and don't stress." Gina gently squeezed my arm. "We'll find someone here."

It wasn't that I couldn't fight, I was a skilled fighter, but finding my mate was front and center. I'd gone too long without one by my side. After so many years of being alone it was time I found him. I'd had partners, but none made my blood boil, none powerful enough to make me want to lose myself with him. And I wanted to get lost, I needed to, dammit.

Shouldn't every women find their perfect partner? I thought so.

We readied ourselves to the best we could under the circumstances, finished the bottle of wine and opened the door when someone knocked.

The females left the safety of their rooms and stood in a neat line by the door. We were waiting for the alphas to be seated.

Chapter Four

SHAWN

Each Alpha sat in their respective seats. They spaced us about 3 feet apart while the moving walkway looped around us.

Nick found his name badge on the seat right in front. The alpha who sat behind him wouldn't see a thing, so he asked the night manager, Valerie, if he could move to the back. He didn't mind moving. It would be better for him to see the ladies from the back instead of right in front. And, as he had said with a sly grin, he didn't want to scare them off just yet.

Dim torches adorned the walls while soft harp music played. The air was cool against my face while my body heated. A nervousness swept through me as I pulled on the collar of my dress shirt. I sipped from my drink which did nothing to calm me.

Each alpha sat in comfortable chairs with a small table large enough for a bowl of nuts and a drink. I sat somewhere in the middle, on the far right-hand side with an alpha from Salt Lake City to my left.

During the brief trip down to the Ballroom, the others were quiet with a nervous energy. That energy only intensified the longer we sat with only our thoughts keeping us occupied. The alpha from Salt Lake City kept stealing glances in my direction and tugged on his collar.

We waited until ten minutes after six when the doors at the back of the Ballroom finally opened. They changed the music to something lively yet tasteful, and the surrounding air felt electrified. The nervous energy vibrated with anticipation.

The females entered.

"Good evening, ladies and alphas. Welcome to Wolf Retreat. I am your night manager, Valerie, and I'm sure you are all eager to get started. This preliminary step is for the alphas to see the females before dinner, and before our first activity." Valerie's voice was loud over the music without deafening us. She introduced the first female along with their hometown, likes and dislikes. There were fifteen females in total.

Valerie introduced each female then abruptly stopped. I'd only counted thirteen females she introduced and wondered what happened to the other two.

The women moved along the walkway at a slow pace. A mixture of the various perfumes left in their wake as they disappeared behind us. Some were pretty and some average looking. There was a mixture of body types and skin tones. Each stunning in their similar ballgowns, which I suspected the company had sponsored. If the females attended for free, I doubted they needed to splurge on unnecessary items such as a ballgown.

'None of them we want,' mumbled Beast.

'At least you're up. Are you going to help, lazy wolf.' I whispered

my thoughts back to my other more dangerous half, my beast, the one who needed to claim our fated mate.

'All I smell is perfume,' he grumbled and stretched lazily.

I sighed inwardly as I raked my gaze up and down the women.

'There are only thirteen—' I stated, my thoughts cut short when heels slapping against the tile echoed inside the Ballroom. Someone was running, actually two someone's. I turned around to see who it was, and all I saw was the big guy turning around.

At first I saw nothing, then two women came into view. My heart raced as I watched them step onto the platform, then the moving walkway.

Nick fidgeted in his seat as he stared open-mouthed, and I couldn't help smiling. He liked one of them already. *Good for you,* I thought. I turned around in time for number thirteen to pass me.

"And slightly delayed are two females from Krystal Creek," Valerie's voice boomed in the Ballroom. I turned toward the women as they moved closer. It reminded me of the request I'd received from the WAA about Krystal Creek and the issues they'd experienced with a rogue pack killing their alpha. It was a smart move on their part to be here, but I couldn't help feeling like a failure. I was so caught up in my personal business I hadn't responded to the request. My jaw muscles ticked at my incompetence. If they didn't find their mate here, I'd do everything in my power to protect their pack.

Valerie continued with the introductions for the women. The first one, Gina, had delicate features in a faerie sort of way. She was part fae, part wolf, and even her hair shimmered silver. She was pretty—

'But she's not our type,' added Beast.

'No, she's not our type.'

The woman behind Gina, Carmen, was tall, lean—

"Carmen may be the oldest female we've hosted before, but as you can see, she's lovely…"

I furrowed my brows at Valerie's comment and would love to slap the rest of her words out of her mouth if it didn't get me kicked out and banned. I didn't think it was necessary to mention Carmen's age, forty, when she was trying to find her mate. In hindsight, forty wasn't even that old. But in wolf packs, they may consider it slightly old. It made me wonder why she hadn't found her mate until I remembered I too hadn't found mine and I was pushing fifty.

It was a good thing the wolf gene slowed our aging process; we could be sixty and still be as fit as a thirty year old.

Regardless of her age, Carmen was stunning; her shoulder length black hair and emerald-colored eyes sparkled. Her face thin and features delicate. I could tell she looked after her body because it was just, *wow*. My mouth was dry and my heart stuttered in my chest. I shifted uncomfortably in my seat as I adjusted my erection to one side.

'Hmmm,' stirred beast

'Do you like her?'

'Maybe.'

'Me too.'

The longer I stared at this raven beauty, the harder my dick pressed against my zipper. Mr. Boston behind me whistled low and dirty and I dared not glance over my shoulder because if I saw him gawking at Carmen, I might smash my fist into his face.

The thought took my breath away. I reached for the

glass and downed the whiskey. The cold liquid burned the back of my throat, forcing a cough.

A low rumbling growl sounded from the back, and I knew it was Nick without having to glance in that direction.

Christ, were all the alphas after Carmen. If they were, I'd have to sharpen my skills and fight for what I wanted.

'We will do what it takes to make Carmen ours.'

'That's if she wants us, Beast.'

'I'm happy to do the caveman style, and club her over the head.'

I chuckled at Beast's thoughts. Maybe...

I couldn't keep my eyes off Carmen as she passed me. All I wanted was a chance for her to get to know me, then we could decide where to go from there.

"Alphas, please move to the dining room behind you," Valerie said once all the females had left. "We've placed the ladies at certain tables, but if you would like to be seated beside a particular female, all you have to do is ask."

I waited for the alphas to leave, then slowly stood, thinking about ledgers and accounting and not the woman in green. Once happy that I wasn't flashing a hard-on, I followed the rest into the dining area.

When Valerie came into view, I flagged her down. "Is anyone sitting with Carmen?"

Valerie's dark eyes sparkled, and her smile split her face in two. "She is, but if you like I can ask her to accompany you?"

"Please," I said, nodding curtly, and approached the table with my name on it.

Chapter Five

CARMEN

Trust Gina to make us late when we were within walking distance of the venue. She was nervous and needed her gum. I allowed her to chew on it for ten seconds, then forced her to spit it out.

Not only were we late, I almost fell. Now I was sweaty, my skin cold, and my cheeks heated when we burst through the doors.

Valerie's shrill voice boomed, making me flinch. Then when she said my age, I wanted to ram my fist into her face. Usually, I wasn't a violent person, but I'd gladly slap her face and knew it would make me feel better.

"Don't worry about it," Gina whispered as we moved onto the walkway.

I squeezed the hand she offered and plastered on a smile while my eyes pricked. I would enjoy this retreat even if I didn't find my forever partner. It saddened me to still be single, but I was not alone. I had friends who were my chosen family.

The alphas sat in the middle of the horseshoe shape the

walkway made and half were heart-pounding, wet-panty gorgeous. There were different types of alphas; tall, dark, and dangerous type. The flaming red-head with piercing green eyes type. The blond who had an impressive body— from what I could tell—but his face didn't do it for me. He wasn't ugly, more nondescript. It's awful of me to say that about a man's face, but that's what I saw first. Face, body, and then the hidden gem between his legs—in that order. But what sold me was his personality, as cliche as it sounded it was true. He could be bad, dangerous, but a complete dick. No, I wanted someone who possessed a bit of each quality. Was that too much to ask? Probably. It could be the reason my mate hadn't revealed himself yet. I had raised my bar too high and most struggled to reach it even on their tiptoes.

We were at the halfway mark when something caught my attention. An alpha, third row from the front with dark hair, dark stubble, drowning blue eyes, and all in a neatly packaged suit. I felt his dark gaze rake up my body as if he was the one doing the touching. My skin burned where he looked and I wished I could fly away.

His eyes lingered on my chest and was sure he could see my hard nipples through the gown, but I was too afraid to break contact. If I blinked would he disappear like he was a figment of my overactive imagination? I stared at him, no; I gawked—bordering on ogled like a lecherous tart.

As we moved past his seat, his glacial-blue eyes finally met mine and entranced me. The man could not stop staring at me. I prayed it was a good sign.

"Carmen!" Someone yelled in time for me to see the walkway ending and I stepped onto the platform instead of crashing face first to the ground.

"Thanks, Gina," I said to my friend who waited for me near the door.

She mumbled something, but she wasn't giving me attention. I followed her line of sight and saw what she was staring at. The alpha was huge; easily the biggest man I'd ever seen, and I wondered what his wolf looked like.

"Walk through ladies." Valerie brought us out of our trance and ushered us through the doors and into the dining room. "Look for your name cards and have a seat. The alphas will be with you shortly."

"Did you see that guy?" Gina whispered near my ear. "Oh my gods, I think my ovaries just exploded."

I burst out laughing. When I contained myself, I added. "And he's handsome. Did you see the one with the black hair?"

"Huh? Which one? Sorry, all I saw was Gigantor at the back," she grinned, wiggling her eyebrows. Her eyes glazed over as if the sight of the alpha had switched off her brain.

One would think we'd never seen alphas before. But there was something different about the one with black hair I couldn't put my finger on, or rather I'd like to put my finger on that alpha. I shook away the dirty thoughts.

"Never mind. I see you're over there." I pointed to Gina's table and walked around looking for my name. "Behave," I warned and left her, a quivering puddle waiting to be claimed.

I giggled as hope rose within me. If Gina found her mate here and the dark and lovely alpha felt the same way about me, then the chance of our pack succeeding increased.

"Carmen," Valerie said as she approached. "Shawn from Sterling Meadow has asked for your company," she said, pointing at the dark and yummy alpha seated at his table—staring at me.

"Thanks," I said, turned and slowly approached.

My pulse thundered in my ears as a nervousness swept through my body like a grade school crush. It was ridiculous to feel like this. I always thought love at first sight was for fools, yet here I was with my heart in my throat and my palms clammy. I dared not wipe my hands on my gown and picked up the napkin near the seat Shawn had pulled out for me.

"Carmen, my name is Shawn, and I'd be humbled if you'd join me for dinner," he said. His voice velvety smooth with rough edges and I shook his hand. A zap of electricity shot up my arm as we touched. A small gasp tore from my lips and when I glanced up at him he stared wide eyed as if he'd felt it too.

"That was unexpected," he said as he pushed my chair in and sat beside me. "You're from Krystal Creek," he stated. "I heard about the troubles you've been experiencing."

Perhaps I was the only one who had felt something more when our hands touched. I thought I'd finally found someone, but he only wanted to dine with me to speak about our alpha troubles. I recalled what Valerie had said when she told me Shawn wanted me to join him for dinner —he was from Sterling Meadow. In my excitement I hadn't realized who he was. We'd asked for his help. I knew it was too good to be true.

"Yes," I said, staring at my hands.

"Do you know who the rogue wolves are?"

"From what I gathered, their pack kicked them out and now they're looking for a new one." I turned my body to face him and looked him in the eye. I needed to put my sensitivities behind me. We needed help, and perhaps Shawn was the one to do just that. "When they came across our pack, they saw a simple way in. Their alpha is powerful," I said, and swallowed hard. The back of my throat ached as I recalled watching John's face explode by the steel fists of the rogue wolf. It was awful to watch and I was sure some of the younger females would suffer from PTSD.

As I told Shawn the details of that awful day, concern reflected in his cool-blue eyes. His expression was that of a brother needing to help a fellow wolf out. When I ended the story, I couldn't help the sinking feeling of my hopes dashed at finding my mate, but elated that he might help us.

Before Shawn responded, our starters arrived, a seafood dish. We ate in silence and sipped on our wine.

Shawn finished first and leaned against the chairback. He seemed to fight something when he finally turned his gaze on me.

"I don't know what it is about you, Carmen. But..." he seemed to struggle with the words and cleared his throat. "I may set myself up for failure, so tell me what you think. I really like you, and I want to get to know you," he smiled, then added. "And my beast seems to like you, too."

My heart jumped into my mouth, and I couldn't respond. I smiled and was sure it was one of those silly goofy smiles. I swallowed the lump and said. "I'd love that."

Chapter Six

SHAWN

After the awkward introduction, dinner flew by. Wine flowed freely and conversation became easy. Carmen was pleasant to speak with. But I hardly concentrated on what she was saying and more how she said it. I kept staring at her emerald green eyes, then down the slope of her dainty nose and lingered on those full lips. Lips I wanted all over my body.

My palm itched to touch every inch of her skin. Instead, I reached for her long dark strands, catching glimpses of purple highlights I wasn't sure if they were natural. I liked the two tones; it suited her.

Watching her lips move as she spoke and then how her smile brightened her face. I had held back for as long as I could. When I couldn't resist anymore, I cupped one side of her face. She leaned into my hand and closed her eyes. The affection she afforded shot straight to my chest, warming me from within.

'We like her,' Beast whispered in my head. *'Make her ours.'*
'We should at least get to know her.'

He scoffed at my response and growled.

"Are you okay?" Carmen asked, bringing me out of my silent conversation with Beast.

"Fine, why?"

"It looked like you went somewhere for a second."

"Just speaking with my animal."

"Oh," she said, her interest piqued and shuffled her chair closer. "Do tell." She placed her elbows on the table and her chin in her palms, and batted her eyelashes.

Carmen was a pure were-wolf and had her own she-wolf to manage. She understood what I was going through; the internal banter. But whether to tell her how Beast truly felt was another thing.

"I'm serious, Shawn, I want to know," she said, her demeanor shifting to serious, and sat back with her hands in her lap—waiting.

I could lie. But I didn't want to. I didn't want our relationship to start off with lies and so I told her. "Beast wants you, Carmen," I blurted, waiting for the backlash.

Carmen didn't respond. She blinked rapidly as she mulled over the words. And something told me I might have messed up my chance. My heart stuttered and hoped I didn't break it before we even made her ours.

I was about to apologize when she shook her head to shush me and stood. Craning my neck up to see where she was going, but she didn't leave. I hadn't scared her away... yet. Placing her hand on my shoulder, the heat from her palm burned, but I welcomed it. It was the tingly feeling that sat right with me and made Beast stretch and yawn like a lazy-ass wolf.

Carmen surprised me by pulling up her gown high enough to raise her right leg over my lap and sat down, straddling me. Her heated core burned my crotch area, and

I breathed in her scent. It was unmistakable; lavender and something else I couldn't place... her arousal?

Oh gods.

She reached for my neck, her palms burning my skin near my ears, and slithered her hands down until they settled on my shoulders and leaned in to one side. "I'd love that," she purred near my ear, her fiery breath beating against my neck causing my arms to pebble.

Beast howled, then grumbled in my chest. He was happy.

I gripped her hips in response and pulled her closer so she could feel my excitement, then cupped her face and brought her closer. Our lips barely touched yet desire lingered, not just from me but her too. She stared at me with hooded eyes, her pupils dilated and her breath coming in quick breaths.

We closed the gap, our lips crashing against each other, then our tongues tasted the other. She still tasted of dessert and I couldn't get enough of her.

Beast howled again, sniffing the surrounding air as if he sensed her wolf and bark-howled. He'd never done that before, and it made me happier. We'd found our fated mate.

Carmen's hands roamed across my chest and shoulders until she wrapped her arms around my neck, not letting go.

We kissed until forced to stop, coming up for air. Both breathless and wanting more. Not wanting to give the others a show, I brought her in for an embrace, never wanting to let go. The urgency of claiming her as ours was greater and the sooner we took care of that the sooner we could live our lives.

"We hope you enjoyed dinner," Valerie's voice boomed in the hall, tearing everybody away from their conversations.

Carmen lifted her leg to climb off, but I stopped her and shook my head. "You're not going anywhere, babe," I said and shifted her into a seated position with both legs across my lap and her body resting against the right side of my chest. She leaned into me, resting her head against mine, and I squeezed her thigh.

"Before anybody rushes off. We have an activity for the night."

"I must be honest, I don't feel like doing this." Carmen stared at me with pleading eyes. Her expression told me one thing, bed… now!

I smiled knowingly; I felt the same. As I glanced around the room, Nick had Gina on his lap too. They were kissing and cuddling and I wondered whether they'd matched or if it was just an attraction.

Two alphas seemed engrossed with their dates and doubted neither wanted to do this activity either.

When I caught sight of the alpha from Nashville, with a female on either side of him, he sat with his arms folded and stared directly at me. Then his eyes darted to Carmen, and a possessiveness I'd never felt before flooded me. I pulled Carmen closer, alerting her to my discomfort, and she followed my line of sight.

"He gives me the creeps," she whispered. "When we were on that walkway thing, his hard stare made me feel naked. I didn't like it. Even Gina said he frightens her. And he has two females yet he stares at me." She shuddered and tucked her head into the nape of my neck.

"If you'll please follow me and I'll explain what's required." Valerie's voice boomed.

"We can leave, just say the word and we're gone," I said and helped Carmen to her feet, then stood beside her. I reached for her hand and we followed the others outside.

"We've noted some Alphas have already found someone they'd like to get to know a little more intimately, and to help you along we've devised a game to get you there quicker." Valerie stood on the edge of the circle we'd made and clapped.

Before I could respond, blue furry hands grabbed Carmen from behind and whisked her away. I snarled at the blue wolf, but before I could retaliate a white light struck me, knocking me on my ass. More white light struck various alphas as more blue wolves took their females.

The only alpha doing nothing was the red-head from Nashville. He snarled, staring at me, then turned his evil gaze toward Carmen and pursued.

My chest ached at the realization that Nashville wanted *my* Carmen. My body felt like I'd been tasered and fought through the pain. Even though my left leg was numb, I climbed to my feet. My leg now like pins and needles stabbing me, and I howled. This prompted the other wolves to howl in response, and we swarmed the blue wolves as one.

I felt heat on my left and found Nick running beside me; his face etched in anger. He was ready to rip these wolves new ones, and I'd gladly help.

"They took my woman," he grumbled. His voice deeper and menacing. He curled his lips over his teeth revealing fangs as they elongated. His eyes glowed blue as fury thrummed through him.

"Did you see Nashville?"

"Yeah, I wouldn't mind removing a limb. I'll even do it with one arm tied behind my back."

"He's mine if he touches Carmen."

Nick nodded in understanding and we ran harder.

I didn't feel the chill in the air, nor the dark surrounding the land. Although my vision was clearer and brighter in my wolf form, my eyesight adjusted fine, but with the surrounding chaos I struggled to find the blue wolves who had taken Carmen. All the bastards dressed the same and there were many. My sense of smell was better as a wolf, and I wondered whether to shift.

"Maybe we should shift?" Nick said, sensing my discomfort. But before I answered, clothing rained down on us as fur flowed over his body in one swift motion. Nick was a giant brown wolf that could pass as a freaking bear. This guy was massive and easily double my size. I was glad to have him on my side.

Without thinking, I ripped my clothing off and leapt into the air. White/brown fur covered my muscular body as I shifted, no longer feeling any pain as my transition throughout the years became seamless. I knew my eyes glowed yellow in this form, and Beast growled as we sniffed the air in search of our mate.

The scent of the blue wolves masked the scent of Carmen, but I followed the general direction they'd taken her. Her smell had already imprinted into my brain, and I'd never forget her lavender scent until the day I died.

A wolf howled in pain up ahead. Nick and I bolted in the direction, praying it wasn't one of our females.

Chapter Seven

CARMEN

The moment blue claws gripped me by the arms, my heart tugged and stuttered in my chest. They were taking me away from my mate and risking my pack. Although I heard Valerie say it was *only* a game, I didn't like it. Being kidnapped by blue wolves was not fun and being wolf-handled worse. It reminded me of that rogue pack who'd threatened our younger females, and myself.

The only thought swarming inside my head was I couldn't allow that to happen. Not again. A surge of adrenaline coursed through my veins, along with the power within, and I swiveled in Blue Wolf's embrace and shoved my palm up his partially shifted face. His jaw was still human but his blue fur covered the sides of his head like thick sideburns and his ears were in his wolf form.

The hit to his jaw angered him and he tugged harder on my arm.

"Let go of me!" I screamed and punched his jaw when another blue wolf grabbed my other arm.

"Don't fight us, Miss. We don't want to hurt you. It's only a *game*."

"I don't care and I don't appreciate being wolf-handled."

"Stop or it will force us to subdue you," Blue Wolf on my left growled his threat.

I wasn't a damsel in distress. And I wasn't about to act like it for the sake of an activity. These blue wolves worked for the company and it was their job. But I didn't like being taken away from the man I'd waited so long to meet. He could help keep my pack together and out of the claws of the rogues. There was no way I'd allow these idiots to hold me against my will.

The two blue wolves pulled me into a dark corner near a copse that surged with their power. Glitter sparkled near my eyes as a thin film surrounded us. I reached out to pop the film that shimmered with a silky substance, but Blue Wolf on my left swatted my hand away.

"What?"

"Don't touch or I'll restrain you," he warned, arching a black eyebrow. He too had partially shifted with blue sideburns and wolf-ears and his arms covered in blue fur that ended with very large, sharp claws.

"What are you guys? I've never heard of blue wolves before?"

"We're part fae, and our tribe live in these mountains." Blue Wolf on my right motioned at the dark land behind us.

"How convenient for the company to have you in their employ."

"Employ?" Blue Wolf on my right scoffed as if it were a swear word. "More like forced."

"Shut up," Blue Wolf on my left chastised his buddy.

"Don't they pay you? Are you their pet?" I asked carefully. I wasn't sure what was going on, but it didn't seem like they enjoyed their job and I wondered how the company forced them to work.

When silence answered my question, I thought it best not to poke the angry blue wolf and instead focus on how to get away from them. I stared at the strange silky gateway keeping me here and wondered if it hurt to go through it.

"Will it hurt?"

Blue Wolf on my right glanced at me.

"This," I pointed at the magical barrier, "or is it just to hide us?"

"To hide," Blue Wolf on my left said.

As I was about to test their reflexes, something caught my eye. The alpha from Nashville approached. He stared right at me. His green eyes held dark secrets I did not want to know. I held my breath, willing him to disappear. He blinked and turned away. Exhaling a shaky breath, I stood behind Blue Wolf on my left. He sensed my discomfort and stood in front of me, but kept hold of my hand. I relaxed slightly. The last thing I wanted was Nashville touching me.

In that moment, all I heard was my steady breathing. I barely registered the blue brutes near me. The sound of insects seized. The wind no longer caressed the trees surrounding us, and it felt as though I was being watched.

Both wolves stared ahead, so it wasn't them, but something strange was happening. My arms pebbled, and a cold shiver ran down my back. On instinct, I glanced up. My scream caught in my throat. Nashville dropped soundlessly behind me, gripped me with my arms to my side and yanked backward. The two wolves were slow to react. The momentum of pulling them with me too great and they smashed into each other.

Nashville yanked to the left and howled. "You're my

prize, darlin',", he drawled, his hot sour breath against my neck left me nauseated.

"Let me go," I said through gritted teeth.

"No," he said and licked my neck.

I froze, waiting for him to sink his teeth into me. When nothing else happened, instinct took over. The power of many coursed through my veins and I smashed my head against his. The distinct sound of a bone cracking echoed around us, and Nashville let go of me. I spun around to see him doubled over to nurse his broken nose and I kneed him in the face. He roared in pain, standing up.

To get away from him, I needed him down longer than a second. With that thought, I kicked him in the nuts and bolted in the opposite direction, heading toward the lights.

More blue wolves ran in different directions, each with a female, as the alphas pursued. Shouting echoed behind me as a blue wolf approached, asking where I was going. I ran away from him, toward the darkest area. When the girl pulled out of his hold, he ignored me and chased after the girl.

I ran behind a large boulder and hid. My chest heaved as I sucked in air, my skin damp but cold. A shudder ran through me as I wiped the slick wetness from my neck, dinner threatening to come back up at the thought of Nashville touching me. If he touched me again, I would claw his eyes out. Why did some men think they could act all caveman-like? No woman in her right mind thought smashing a girl over the head and dragging her by her hair a romantic gesture. It was barbaric. And those days were long over. If I saw him again, I'd tell him to 'use your words.' Asshole.

The chaos behind me continued. Women yelling then bouts of laughter filled the air. I turned to my far left and saw two naked bodies moving as one, followed by heavy breathing. I was happy for them but sheesh. Some might see this as a fun exercise, but I wasn't enjoying it at all.

I understood why the company did this. It acted like a catalyst to speed up the bonding. If there were two who might like each other, by taking one away it forced the male into possessive mode and take what was his. No wonder their success rate was so high.

When a large white wolf ran past, I swallowed hard. Not sure who he was but tried desperately not to bring unwanted attention to myself. The wolf stopped, sniffed the air and turned around; his glowing yellow eyes stared straight at me and he approached.

My heart started beating rapidly and was sure it was about to burst through my chest. I tried to meld into the rock behind me but it was too late, he'd seen me. The wolf scent marked me, sniffed near the area where Nashville had licked, growled and proceeded to lick over it. The sensation wasn't as sickly as Nashville and the area tingled. It was as if this wolf marked his territory over Nashville's. He sat down, and stared at the chaos behind me.

I didn't know which alpha he was, but since he wasn't trying to capture or eat me, I didn't run away again.

As the evening progressed, the noises behind me lessened as I assumed the alphas found their females. My mind wandered to Shawn and his powerful hands squeezing my hips. The thoughts of him left my heart racing and I could finally understand what the fuss was all about. To find your true love, your mate, was something unique to each.

I peered over the boulder and saw no more blue wolves running around, nor did I see Nashville.

Since my thoughts were already on Shawn, I wondered what had happened to him. I side-glanced the white wolf now on his stomach, still watching those behind me. That couldn't be him, could it?

"Shawn?" I whispered.

The wolf's ears perked up. Now sitting, he whined softly.

"Hi," I smiled and scooted closer. "Why didn't you say something sooner?" I asked but he said nothing. Instead he stared at me with those golden eyes, boring into my soul. "This was a terrible activity."

He snarled, baring his sharp canines.

"Yeah, you could say that again." I shuddered thinking about what the company would make us do tomorrow.

Shawn growled, his hackles raised. Footsteps neared, and someone shone a bright beam on Shawn's furry face, making him snarl violently. My arms pebbled as his power struck me.

"The activity is over. You can return to your rooms," the voice said, then the light disappeared, and the footsteps moved away from us.

"Thank goodness," I said, crouching over the boulder to see the other side. We were the only ones outside. "I guess it's over." I stood and scratched behind Shawn's ear as he rubbed against my leg.

We traversed side by side until we passed the area where the blue wolves had kept me when another wolf jumped on top of me, knocking me to the ground. My face smashed into the dirt, tasting sand and coughed.

Shawn didn't hesitate, he jumped pushing the other wolf off me. They snarled, howled, and snapped at each other.

A blue wolf approached, helping me to my feet, and called for help on his radio.

I didn't know who the brown wolf was but suspected

Nashville; he was not happy I'd given him blue balls as a reward for shitty behavior.

The brown wolf tried to get to me again, but Shawn wouldn't allow it. Every time Nashville tried to run around him, Shawn snapped his larger jaw. Shawn was much bigger than the brown wolf and I suspected he knew this and didn't want to fight Shawn, but his hate for me seemed to fuel his anger—or stupidity.

As more partially shifted blue wolves appeared, the brown wolf gained confidence and lurched at me. Shawn was quicker, intercepted and knocked the brown wolf to the ground. Before he got up, Shawn bit into his neck keeping him in place.

"That's enough," Valerie shouted behind us, but Shawn didn't let go.

"The brown wolf started it," I said, pointing at them. I felt like a kid in class telling the teacher who stole the cookie.

"Tear them apart," she commanded. "Or I'll tranquilize them." Her tone was cold as she raised the dart gun, aiming it at Shawn.

Two blue wolves reached for Shawn who let go of Nashville's neck, snapped at the blue wolves and ran out of their grasps to stand near me. Two more blue wolves approached Nashville, who howled and nursed his wounds. Unfortunately, he was a fast healer and his skin started knitting together.

When Nashville stood on four paws, his menacing gaze found me and I just about wet myself. He was beyond pissed.

"I hate it when this happens," Valerie said through a deep sigh. "Unfortunately, both alphas are banned. Please collect your things and leave."

Chapter Eight

SHAWN

I shifted into my human form with ease, albeit tiredly. Carmen stood back while I changed but neared once I was in the flesh; wearing an enormous grin. Her eyes kept darting below my waist but I didn't mind, she could stare all she wanted or touch. I'd love her hands on me.

I pulled her into my side as we watched Nashville shift into his human form.

Carmen caressed, then slapped my ass and wrapped her arms around my waist. I rewarded her action with a kiss on her head.

"Nashville," I glowered. "Come near us again and I'll kill you."

"The bitch kicked me."

"You deserved worse," I said, turning us around and heading back toward the hotel. "Now that I have to leave... I don't suppose you want to come home with me."

Her contagious grin warmed my chest. "Absolutely, but—"

"I haven't forgotten about your pack," I reminded her.

"And I will protect all of you. Whether your pack joins mine, or I send my second to Krystal Creek. You will all be safe."

Carmen hugged tighter. My erection grew larger and I couldn't wait to make her mine.

As much as I wanted to bed Carmen, this wasn't the place to do it. She deserved privacy and a little romance. We'd have our fun back home.

It was four in the morning by the time I'd packed my bag in my truck and leaned against it, waiting.

Carmen agreed to drive back with me, but first we'd stop at her pack to assess the situation and let them know of our plans.

Nick exited with his bags, wearing a cheesy grin.

"What bird did you eat?"

"Oh man, that Gina lights my fire," he said, rubbing his chest. "That girl just does it for me," he winked darkly.

I was happy for the big guy. At least things worked out for him and me. "Then why are you leaving?"

"Carmen is leaving and Gina doesn't want to stay without her friend. And besides, she only wants me." He chuckled, the sound like rolling thunder.

"Do you know about the rogue pack who wants to fight their new alpha."

"Yeah, and I think I can take them."

Although the pack wasn't mine to defend, a sting of jealousy hit me that Nick wanted to fight them, and possibly lead the pack. I couldn't disagree with him, and I didn't want to fight him for it. I wondered what he'd do with the pack when he won.

"Are you going to move to Krystal Creek or bring Gina to Atlantis?"

"She'll fly back with me when everything is settled. There's no way I'm giving up Atlantis. Besides, her pack is tiny compared to mine and they're all welcome to join us."

"Does Gina know?"

He nodded unconvincingly.

I wanted to ask more questions when the girls approached, their smiles broad as they spoke while staring at us. I couldn't bring myself to crush their happiness. They'd soon find out what their future held, whether with me or with Nick.

Beast stirred when he smelled Carmen nearby. He was elated she was driving with us.

I watched my raven haired beauty, and still couldn't believe we'd found each other at a retreat of all places when our towns were so close.

This time the rumbling was my stomach. I didn't bother eating again after my shifting and would grab something along the road. Right now, all I wanted was my girl, and to get home.

Beast growled in my head; unsure why, I turned toward the hotel and Nashville exited. He gave me the finger, climbed into his corvette and sped away.

"Asshole," Carmen yelled, giving him the finger. She threw her bag in the back and leaned against my side. I pulled her closer and kissed the top of her head. She turned, pressing her body against mine, rocked onto her toes and wrapped her arms around my neck.

"Kiss me," she breathed seductively.

I spun us around, crushed her between me and my truck. The feel of her soft breasts against my chest fueled my hunger and the need to get home to spend *quality* time alone.

She moaned as she swept her tongue inside my mouth, tracing along my teeth when my canines elongated. She whimpered as our kiss intensified, our bodies heating the longer we touched.

When I finally pulled away, she was breathless. My nostrils flared when I caught the scent of her arousal with a hint of lavender.

"I don't think I can wait until I get to the Wolf Pack," I moaned.

"Maybe we find a place along the way," she said with a salacious wink, sashayed toward the passenger door and blew me a kiss as she climbed inside.

"Christ, you're gonna kill me." I adjusted myself to a more comfortable position. "Maybe we'll see you at their clubhouse," I said to Nick.

"Yep, see you there buddy," Nick said, pulling away in his rental with Gina following him in her car.

Chapter Nine

CARMEN

We were on the open road, the views of the mountains spectacular, and the conversation flowed. At first glance, Shawn seemed like the type of wolf with a stick up his butt; very serious, quiet, yet dangerous. Like a cobra waiting to strike. The more we spoke, the more he relaxed and showed me his real side.

"Don't you find it strange we came all the way here to meet when our towns are so close?" I asked, my hand firmly on his lap.

Shawn raised my hand to his lips and kissed my knuckles. The sensation of his soft lips against my skin shot fireworks through my arm and to my core. I squirmed in my seat from how he affected me. He grinned knowingly.

"Well," he said and placed my hand back on his thigh so he could continue driving. "Life works in mysterious ways. I hardly leave Sterling Meadow and I doubt you leave your town either?"

"You're right, I hardly go anywhere. Whether it's

because I don't drive or because everything I need is around me I'll never know. Perhaps it's a combination of it all."

"So we wouldn't have met, anyway. It's as if the world forced us to leave our town and meet at the retreat."

"I just can't believe it took me so long. It was only the threat to our pack that made me realize I needed to do something. I always thought I'd end up a spinster and an aunt to the pups. I never had the drive of becoming a mother. And I've been in my town forever, but…" I stared at Shawn while he drove; at his dark features, neatly kept hair and trimmed beard. His jaw muscles ticked, waiting for my answer. "But I'd move for you. When I know my pack is safe, I'm all yours."

Shawn howled deep and throaty, and I knew my response pleased his Beast. My wolf pushed to the surface and sniffed the air. She smelled his wolf, and she liked it.

"My wolf senses yours is around. He likes her and can't wait to run in the metaphysical realm."

"Mine too," I smiled at Shawn like a love-sick puppy.

My thoughts came to a crashing halt when I saw a corvette heading for us. It approached Shawn's side of the truck. They were going to T-Bone us and strike Shawn first. My reflexes were too slow to warn Shawn, on instinct I reached for his steering wheel and yanked right.

The other car crashed into us, metal scraping against metal. Because of the sudden change in direction, the other vehicle didn't strike Shawn's door, instead smashing into the body of the truck. Shawn slammed into me but kept my hand in his. My head crashed into my window and before the impact shot me out the windscreen, Shawn pulled me into the curve of his body. His lightning fast reflexes and powerful hands kept me from kissing shards of glass and possible decapitation.

We should've worn our seatbelts, it was the safe thing to do. But we didn't.

The truck rolled a few times, but being cocooned with Shawn saved me as we bounced around the inside. When our vehicle finally came to a stop, we had settled in the back seat. On our sides, our limbs entwined and heads in each other's necks.

My body only pummeled and bruised. I moved each limb and wiggled fingers and toes. Nothing had broken, and I wasn't bleeding. Shawn had saved me.

"Shawn?" I whispered. "You okay?" I nuzzled him onto his back, but his eyes remained closed. He didn't move. I placed my ear near his mouth and my hair faintly tickled my cheek from his barely-there breaths. My chest tightened as the back of my throat ached. "No! This can't be happening. Shawn! Wake up! Please, oh please," I yelled, shaking him. "Don't do this to me. Please wake up."

Someone whistled outside. I froze. Peering out the shattered windows, I couldn't see the person. I only heard them.

"You had to kick me," he drawled.

Nashville. He'd come back to make us hurt. To kill us.

I glanced down at Shawn, still unconscious, and kissed him. "I'm going to get help," I whispered near the shell of his ear, wiped the blood from his neck and felt his faint pulse. He would pull through, just a little battered and bruised. "Don't go anywhere, you hear. I'll be right back," I said and kissed him one last time.

I checked the inside of the truck for anything I could use against this asshole, but saw nothing. I peered through the little back window and saw a tire iron. Once the weapon was in my hand, I crawled out of the truck.

"Nashville," I groaned. "Do you want another kick to the balls?"

"You need to be punished for disobedience."

I harrumphed. "Are you serious? What part of '*I don't like you*', don't you understand?" I kept the tire iron against my leg and out of sight. There needed to be an element of surprise if he attacked first. He was much bigger and stronger than me, and I needed all the help.

"Oh darlin', that never stopped me before." He approached wearing a fat smirk and started unbuckling his belt and unzipped his pants. I didn't like where this was leading, and if he'd done it before it would please me to make him bleed. "But before I kill you, I need to taste that salty skin and take you for a quick spin." He rubbed his erection over his jeans and I shuddered.

I had to time it just right and stood still. I wanted douchebag to think he shocked me so badly I couldn't defend myself.

Honking in the distance distracted Nashville. I raised my hand and brought the tire iron down as hard as I could, striking the soft part between his neck and shoulder. Nashville didn't blink he just crumpled to the ground.

The car drove past as an old woman waved and yelled if we were okay. She was ancient; I didn't need her blood on my hands either. I yelled we were fine and she drove past.

All it took was a moment.

When I felt a heavy body crash into me, knocking out my wind. I knew something bad was happening. This was the end of me. I'd pushed Nashville too far and doubted he liked it when women had the upper hand.

He'd landed on top of me with a hard thud, the tire iron fell out of my hand but before I could reach for it his hands clasped around my neck. Being starved of oxygen was not fun. Blood drained from my head, my eyes bulged as I tried to claw his hands off me.

Remembering the tire iron, I stretched my right hand and felt the cool metal against my fingertips, yet just out of my reach. I touched it with my finger and tried to slide it close enough to pick up; but it only moved slightly. Now caught between my two fingertips, I pulled again.

My head ached. Stars flashed as my vision darkened. Nashville morphed into a gray blur. My hand became numb along with the rest of my body and I died.

Life was ironic; I'd just found my mate when taken away from him. We hadn't even bonded. Regret came to mind; we should've spent the morning together at the hotel before we left. We shouldn't have been in a hurry to leave. If only I did things differently. But things happened, and I'd gladly come back as a ghost to haunt the shit out of Nashville.

When air filled my lungs and my heart raced, I knew something had happened. Was I able to grip the tire iron and smash it into Nashville's head? I didn't know.

My body slowly came alive; I no longer felt cold and moved my toes. I coughed, wheezed and slowly sat up. The ringing in my ears softened and loud thuds and stomps echoed around me. Although my vision was still blurry and my eyes burned I saw movement.

Two figures danced, no, fought before me. I glanced to my right and reached for the tire iron. Shawn must've awoken and danced without me. I'd chat to him once we got rid of the roadkill.

I used the totaled car to climb to my feet and leaned against it. Although I could see better, my eyes still stung like a mother… and my chest ached. I needed more air and breathed deeply.

Shawn smashed his fist into Nashville's face, rocking his head backward. Before Nashville fell to the ground, Shawn pumped his left hook into his jaw. Crunching bones sounded, followed by blood spraying onto the road. Shawn straddled Nashville's chest and continued hitting his face.

All I could manage was to stare at Shawn; his eyebrows pulled down together, his lips pursed, and the veins in his neck and arms stuck out as he took his anger out on Nashville's face. He was going to kill him. I knew I should stop him, but I couldn't. Nashville was going to do things to me, then kill me. He deserved to hurt.

Movement caught my eye when another car pulled up. Nick, the largest man I'd ever seen, bolted out of his car and headed in our direction. I wondered where they'd disappeared to since they had left before us. One glance at Gina's messy hair and glowing cheeks; they'd *stopped* somewhere. I would've high-fived her but now wasn't the time.

Nick lifted Shawn off Nashville's lifeless body and held him firmly in place. "What the fuck, man? What happened?"

"Asshole T-Boned us, and I awoke to find him choking Carmen. If I didn't get him off her, he was going to kill her," Shawn said. His words harsh and angry, yet filled with pain. He turned to me, shoved Nick away from him and ran toward me. "Are you okay? Christ, your eyes." Shawn fretted over me, checking no bones had broken, and cupped my face as he stared at me. We gazed into each other's eyes, each assessing the other's damage. We would be okay, and we would heal. We'd get through this.

"I'm okay," I said hoarsely. My throat hurt even though I swallowed a gallon of spit and blood. Nashville had almost crushed my larynx; lightly touching my neck hurt. "He won't stop coming after me," I said with pleading eyes.

Shawn understood and turned to face Nick. "He's going to kill her, man. We have to do something." He motioned toward the lifeless body. "Is he still alive?"

Now that I could see better, Gina approached with a jacket and covered me. "Your clothing's torn," she whispered as she closed the coat. I glanced down at my torn shirt and unfastened jean button; that was close.

Gina seemed spooked. The pink glow from her cheeks replaced with pale skin. She chewed on her bottom lip as she assessed the carnage on the road and the blood… and then me. I worried for her and didn't want her to stress.

"Thank you," I said and nestled into my friend. Her hug was warm and comforting. It was then I choked up with tears. My emotions ran raw and damaged, yet rage filled my veins. "How are you holding up?"

"I'm fine. I'm worried about you though. You look terrible," she said with a smile. "But still beautiful."

"Thanks, hun." I hugged her tighter as the need to protect her and the pack overwhelmed me. We had Shawn and Nick willing to protect us, but something within called to me.

Nashville moved. I flinched. My beast growled in my head. She wanted to hurt him. If he healed, he wouldn't stop coming for me until I was dead. Or he'd kill Shawn first and then make me watch as he did it. And if he found the other females, he'd damage them too. I couldn't allow him to do any of that. I had to stop him.

I glanced at Shawn and Nick, who seemed to communicate silently.

Nashville groaned, lifted his hand to feel his face. "Bitch!" He mumbled through broken teeth and a thick tongue.

"No!" I yelled, nudged Gina away gently and darted for the bastard on the ground. Raising the tire iron still clutched in my hand, I smashed it into his face then stabbed his chest with it. Blood sprayed my face and body, but I ignored it. My hands ached from the impact and before I could dig the tire iron in again, enormous hands yanked me away, lifted me off the ground and to one side while Nick closed the gap.

"It's okay," Shawn said, turning me away from the carnage. "Shh," he lulled as he set me down and gently wiped blood off my face. "It's okay, babe. I've got you. Why did you do that? I would've done it—"

"I know, but I had to do this... for me. I couldn't allow that bastard to come for us again. He had to hurt. I couldn't allow him to hurt me, you, the pack," I said, my teeth chattering as I shivered.

"Shh, it's okay." He kissed my temple. "I don't think you're weak, babe. You're strong and beautiful, and incredibly dangerous. Just the way I like my woman," he chuckled darkly. His blue eyes twinkled with humor and something akin to pride. "You've been doing everything yourself and for your pack for so long. I understand. Allow me to be there for you. Understand that I'm not going anywhere. And I've got you now, babe," he continued whispering against my temple.

His gentle words were beautiful and struck my heart. The entirety and severity of it all came crashing down. I was a wolf, and I helped protect our pack, but I'd never killed... It was too much. The accident, the attack, the asshole. Then the thought of losing Shawn and the pack struck me like a lightening bolt. It all came crashing down, and I burst into tears. I wrapped my arms around my man's honed body and pressed my ear against his chest. He wrapped his arms around me; his powerful body keeping me close to him was comforting. The smell of Shawn and his wolf eased my soul and calmed my wolf. His heart raced against my face and the soft kisses on my head made the tears fall harder. In that moment it was only the two of us. The rest of the world fell away as I tried to forget what had happened. He held me until I stopped crying and then held me some more.

At least twenty minutes had passed when I relaxed and let go. Reluctantly Shawn released me but kept me close. We turned around and Nashville's body was gone along with most of the debris. Nick and Gina even pushed Shawn's truck to one side.

"I've called for roadside assistance," Nick said, reaching out for Gina's hand, and they stopped near us.

"You okay, hun?" Gina asked.

"Uh-huh," I said, trying my best to sound normal. My throat still ached from Nashville choking me even though I'd started healing. Shawn still looked like he'd gone through a mincer with blood covering his face and body, but his skin had already knitted together. "Where is—"

"No," Nick shook his head. "Don't think about it. He's gone and he'll hurt no one ever again." Nick pinched Gina's ass. "I think we should go, mate. I've left a note on your windscreen. And nobody will find the other vehicle," Nick grinned, turning Gina around. They walked toward Gina's car, but before Nick climbed inside, he threw his car keys at Shawn. "Your things are in my rental. And try to keep up!" he yelled, and Gina's Audi roared to life.

Shawn caught the keys, reached for my hand, and we traversed across the road toward Nick's car. Once inside, I sank into the chair and fastened my seatbelt. My entire body ached and as Shawn drove, I closed my eyes and slept.

Chapter Ten

SHAWN

These last two days had been the busiest ever. My Wolf Pack had never been this hectic before, even with the stuff that had happened in Sterling Meadow. But it was all worth it.

Carmen slept beside me, her mouth open, snoring lightly, and her hand nestled in mine. The vision of her comfortable enough to sleep like that, and in front of me, was endearing and left my heart fluttering.

With only my thoughts to keep me company, the realization of what had transpired hit me. I'd almost lost my person, my mate, my love. And I'd only just found her. I squeezed her hand even though she wouldn't know why, but I would. Beast and I were relieved she was still around and we had time to make her ours.

The two-hour drive went quickly, and the scenery blurred past this time around, and I hadn't wanted to eat. The bloody mess of Nashville's face was enough. I loved flesh, and I loved tearing bloody meat from bones, but to pummel someone's face like that was a first for me.

I hoped Carmen didn't think I was a violent person; I wasn't until someone threatened my pack or my mate. That I couldn't stand for. And to think she killed him by herself. She was strong-willed and stood up for herself, and I respected that—I respected her.

Not sure how she'd blend with my pack, but if her actions were anything to speak of, she'd fit in just fine. I'm sure the WAA would want her, too. I smiled at the thought.

I followed Nick to Krystal Creek and parked beside the Audi.

Carmen stirred. "Are we there yet?"

"Uh-huh." I climbed out the car to get a better look. To say the view surprised me was an understatement. "This is your pack house?" I asked.

Carmen climbed out and nodded. "Yes, home sweet home."

"It's not what I expected." I held my hand out for Carmen, who slipped her smaller hand into mine. "No wonder the rogues want it."

"Nice, huh?"

"It's perfect."

Carmen had told me everybody stayed together in one large building. Since their pack was so small, the 'house' had accommodated everybody. The building was like an apartment complex with an extensive park and beyond that the forest joining up with Sterling Meadow's forest. The suites ranged from one to five bedrooms depending on the family size. She had been in the same one-bedroom apartment since her family left her in town.

We entered the grand foyer and were greeted by a handful of pups with shocked expressions when they saw Nick and then me. Then their frowns turned into smiles as they realized we were here to help. Shouting erupted, followed by laughter. Some pups jumped up and down as they laugh-cried.

Carmen showed me around with Nick and Gina close behind us.

The last room we entered was where some males sat, discussing tactics. When we entered, two young wolves turned weapons on us.

"Easy there," I said, raising my hands. "Do you know how to use those things?" I hated guns. They were a sure death; quick, easy, and the coward's way. And depending on the type of ammunition used, could either maim or kill. Were-animals healed quickly, but not when a bullet struck the heart or head.

I never used guns or knives; apart from my claws. I preferred the satisfaction of hand-to-hand combat.

"Of course we know how to use them." The male closest to me scoffed and rolled his eyes. He was still wet behind the ears and in desperate need of a slap.

Nick rolled his eyes and backhanded the little shit. "Right, when are those rogues coming to pummel your asses to the ground?"

The other male moved farther away from us, cowering on the other side of the room and behind the table.

"They'll be here tomorrow," Carmen said, leaning against me. "Which of you will fight?" She glanced up at me, then at Nick.

Nick shrugged. "I'll go first. If I go down, Shawn's back-up." Then he smiled. "But there's no way I'm going down."

Chapter Eleven

CARMEN

Shawn closed the door behind him and whistled. "Great place," he said. But he wasn't looking at my apartment, he was staring at me. He approached with purpose. I felt like a rabbit trapped with nowhere to go. I stepped backward and into the kitchen island. I dared not to look away. The apex predator ready to pounce.

When he reached me, he cupped my face. And that's all he did. He held me and stared at me. His blue eyes flashed yellow. A low rumbling sound escaped his lips.

The moment I reached for him, his lips crashed on mine. His body touched the line of mine and I felt every toned muscle, and then some.

He dropped his hands to my shoulders, burning their way down my waist and settled on my hips. I yelped when he lifted me onto the island, pushing my legs apart.

"Mine," he growled low and dirty.

My first thought was to hesitate, to stop him, that we should get to know one another first. There was much he needed to know about me; about the things I could do.

That bonding was too soon. But that was a natural response. We only met yesterday, but it felt as if I'd known him my whole life.

My wolf pushed to the surface, sniffing, rolling onto her back, waiting. She liked his wolf; she wanted him.

Shawn's dark gaze shot straight through to my chest, then to my core. Moisture pooled between my legs and I ached to touch him. I wrapped my legs around his waist and pulled him closer. Wanting to feel every inch of him, I reached for his shirt. He stopped me, lowering my hands.

"I know it's soon and that there's so much we need to learn about each other. But... I want to bond here. Now," he said solemnly. "I don't want to wait any longer and tomorrow isn't promised. All we have is this moment." He kissed my knuckles. "Would you do me the honors?" He kept my left hand in his, waiting for my answer.

"There are things we don't know about each other."

"I know but we'll get there. We have our whole lives ahead of us. Please..."

Maybe it was the *'please'* or the desperation in his eyes, but I couldn't deny him. I didn't want to deny him. I wanted to give him everything he wanted, everything he needed. And I'd do so gladly. The last few hours had been scary and filled with tension. We needed a distraction, but more importantly we needed intimacy.

"How gentlemanly of you," I teased, shifting to a lighter tone, and batting my eyelashes. "Why..." I paused, hesitating, or perhaps I wanted to make him sweat.

He froze with my hand stuck to his full lips, his blue eyes pleading.

"Yes!" I pulled his face towards mine again. His hands roamed my body, each touch burned my skin like a branding iron. *Marked.* He pulled on my shirt, broke the kiss and undressed me. When he reached for my bra, I stopped him. "Bedroom?" I said, glancing at the bedroom door.

Shawn scooped me up and carried me to the bedroom, throwing me onto the bed. I bounced once and then he was on top of me, kissing me with urgency. When he realized clothing restricted his access, he climbed off the bed. He reached for his shirt, pulling it off, then his jeans.

I slipped out of my jeans and stood before him in my underwear. He whistled, his gaze raking up my body, and I loved it. I loved how he desired me, and I ached for his touch. When he removed his underwear and his erection sprang free, my cheeks flushed like I was a teenager.

Slowly I slipped off my bra then pushed down my panties. He growled and stalked. I yelped. He leapt on top of me, our mouths found each other and he settled between my legs.

Shawn pulled away and kissed down my neck, sucked on a hard nipple then the other. I flinched when I felt his fangs. Glancing down, he'd given me a love bite on my right breast above my pert nipple.

"Really? What grade are you in?" I joked, then moaned as he bit on the other side.

He ignored me and continued his descent, leaving marks down my waist and on each hip. When he reached the apex of my legs, he pushed my knees up and to the sides, spreading me wide open. I felt exposed and completely vulnerable. But the heated look in his eyes left me wanting him more.

Shawn lowered his head and licked up my slick middle, sucking my folds.

"Fuuuck!" I fell back onto my bed and closed my eyes. I forgot about feeling vulnerable and enjoyed the feel of him, his tongue, his fingers and his heat. He first used one finger, then two as he pumped them into me and I swore at how delicious his technique was.

When I no longer felt his heat, my eyes shot open. Somehow I hadn't realized he was now hovering above me like he was doing a push-up, waiting. When my eyes found his, they glowed yellow.

"I want to claim you, make you mine, but I'm worried," he said, his voice deeper than usual.

"That if you fight, you might lose?"

He nodded.

"Baby, if you fight and they kill you then they might as well kill me, anyway. It's taken me forty-fucking-years to find you. There's no way in hell I'm letting you go. Besides, I won't want to live without you. And if we bond, now, imagine the power you'll gain. Not only from me, but from my pack. We may be small, and we might have more females, but we each have our own strengths—"

He didn't wait for me to finish my thought as he pushed himself inside my heated sheath and I clutched his shoulders like my life depended on it. He rocked into me, unleashing his pleasurable wrath on my body, and I sang for him. My body tensed before the first wave of satisfaction slammed into me, then another. He was relentless, and I loved it. I wanted more.

I'd had lovers, too many to mention, but none like Shawn. And nothing like *this*. Shawn was tender yet fierce. Gentle then consuming. The sensations rocking into me sent sparks throughout my body, I almost felt electrified and about to be consumed by his loving flames.

We'd waited so long to find our mate that we didn't want to wait anymore. We had the rest of our lives to learn everything about each other. Just thinking about spending my life with him left a burning need and my fangs elongated. I felt my wolf as she readied herself to bond with Shawn's wolf. We were ready.

Shawn continued thrusting into me and when our eyes met; at first his eyes filled with pain and suffering. There was no doubt he too thought he'd live a life of solitude, and the thought of losing his pack had been heavy on his shoulders. But now... now he focused on me, eyes glowing, his fangs long and sharp.

"Mine!" He stated gruffly. "Ours!"

To bond fully, we needed to stake our claim with words, then with our body, and lastly with the sharing of blood. We were both purebred wolves, which would result in a firmer bond. If I were human, he'd have given me a choice to change me or I could stay human; in both cases, the bond wouldn't be as potent if two purebreds bonded. We mated for life—or until death. If one of us died, the other would suffer and immediately. Through the other bonds, the partner might survive death. And I would gladly meet him in the metaphysical realm should we die together. I was ready to go to the depths of hell for him.

I nodded. My eyes glowed yellow/green as my wolf howled and I sank my teeth into him.

Shawn didn't hesitate as he bit into the nape of my neck.

His blood was sweeter than I thought, and I swallowed. Shawn's bite was pleasurable and shot straight to my core, sending another orgasm knocking the breath out of me. All the hairs on my body stood straight as a shiver ran down my spine. My heart enlarged as I felt his beast crash into my wolf and they played.

Shawn continued thrusting as our souls shattered and rejoined as one. I whimpered as another delightful wave struck. The sound of my cries fueled Shawn as his actions became uncoordinated. His orgasm hit him and released his heated seed. He stilled and unlatched his fangs from my skin. I did the same, and we licked the wounds.

Shawn fell on top of me, his body glazed with sweat. I unhooked my heels from behind him and lowered my legs.

I felt Shawn's happiness as I was sure he felt mine; like a flower blooming as it matured, so would our bond. Soon we'd be able to communicate telepathically, as if the winds had blown our words to the other.

I felt Shawn's heat, his body, and his heart. Closing my eyes, I sensed others—his pack. My chest rose and fell in time with his as power engulfed us, but not just from our packs, from the earth below us, and from the metaphysical realm.

"Christ, do you feel that?" He breathed as he slid out and off me. He propped himself on his elbow, pulled me into the curve of his body and kept his hand on my stomach, drawing finger circles around my bellybutton. He sucked in deep breaths of air and closed his eyes. "It's so... powerful."

My pulse thundered in my ears and my skin sensitive to his touch. I shivered as waves of goosebumps covered my body.

He kissed my shoulder. I turned onto my side to face him and tucked my head under his chin. A perfect fit.

"This is what it feels like," I said into his chest, planting a delicate kiss near his heart. With our bonding complete, I felt it was more than just that. My body felt alive—*powerful*—the colors brighter, and the feel of Shawn near me soothing. A strength I hadn't known before engulfed us as one, binding us closer.

"I know, if I'd known it would be like this, I would've been persistent," he chuckled, but it sounded hollow.

"The important thing is we found each other."

He kissed the top of my head. "Yes. Speaking of which, nobody knows about you and I want to introduce you to the Wolf Pack."

"Now?"

"Yes, get dressed. But first a shower."

Chapter Twelve

SHAWN

Our shower was just as hot and pleasurable. The more we touched, the closer we bonded. It was indescribable. I felt her emotions; I sensed her insecurities, and I whispered sweet nothings in my mind that left her blushing.

My hand burned where I touched her as if her skin was molten lava and where she caressed, my body felt like sensual energy revitalizing my soul.

I didn't want our time together to end, but we had the rest of our lives together. I wanted to introduce her to my world and even though I didn't need my pack's blessing, it would mean the world to me if they accepted her without my prodding.

We dressed and drove the thirty minutes toward the Wolf Pack in Sterling Meadow. The entire ride there Carmen had her hand on my thigh and drips of power seeped into my skin. The sensation was electrifying, uncomfortable yet perfect. That we still shared growing power was intense, and it left me wondering how much power her pack had.

I parked in my usual spot and led Carmen to the front door. As I opened it, Jason stood like a security guard with his arms folded across his broad chest, wearing a goofy smile.

"Welcome to the family," Jason said, glanced my way for permission and I nodded. He brought Carmen in for a hug that lasted no longer than three seconds.

Beast stirred within my chest, grumbling *'mine'* like a star-crossed lover. I was sure I heard a growl; most likely from me, but power whooshed in my ears that hadn't relented yet.

Carmen wasn't my possession, but I was possessive of her. I didn't want anyone touching her, nor did I want her hurt. Jason knew this since he had just gone through the same thing. He understood. That's why he only hugged for a few seconds.

As we traversed down the long hallway, more wolves greeted us, all showering Carmen with hugs and hand-shakes. Some wolves howled while others clapped. Beast struggled with everyone touching our mate, and I did my best to calm him. The last thing we needed was me tearing into my people.

The welcome home celebration meant the world to me and I was grateful to have such a wonderful pack. I led Carmen outside where an enormous bonfire heated our front. The flames were massive; red, yellow, and streaks of blue licking wood.

"You were expecting us?" I whispered so only Jason heard.

"We all felt it, Shawn," he said with wide eyes. "Your bonding." He jerked his chin in Carmen's direction. "I don't know what kind of wolf she is, but she's powerful. I dare not say potent, but something along those lines."

It never occurred to me to ask Carmen if she had any other powers. Not all wolves had a secondary power other than what came with being a wolf. And it never came up in conversation; there had been no time to discuss. Perhaps that's why she was hesitant to bond, there were things she wanted to tell me.

I squeezed her hand. She turned toward me with a smile that split her face in two and her green eyes glistened. Such a sweet beauty with a mean streak as visions of Nashville bludgeoned and stabbed came to mind.

"Babe," I said, enjoying the pet name roll over my tongue. "Sometimes wolves have additional powers, especially purebreds—"

"And you're wondering if I have any?" She asked carefully.

I nodded.

She glanced up to her left, deep in thought, then finally said. "What's your super power?"

"Fair enough. Apart from my rugged good looks." Carmen grinned and swiped my chest. "I strategize." The lines between her eyes deepened. "I can anticipate my opponent's next moves; like chess. Whether or not I'm thinking about it. It just happens." I suspected it had helped me to remain my pack's leader all these years without having a mate to secure my power.

"But you didn't see Nashville?"

"Nope," I said with frustration laced in my word. "You distract me, babe. How could I not have my head in the clouds with you around?"

She giggled, wrapping her arm around me. "No special power. Did I tell you I was my alpha's second?"

That caught me off guard, and it was my turn to frown. "Then why don't you lead your pack? A woman can

73

become the alpha leader. We don't live in the nineteen hundreds anymore."

"I know, it's just," she said, chewing on her bottom lip and I wanted to chew on that lip now. Actually, I wanted to do more than chew her lip.

"Does your pack respect you?" I asked, she nodded. "Then maybe you must try."

"To be honest, I prefer being second, I don't want to lead."

I could understand, Jason had said the exact same thing. They might have the natural ability, but some didn't want to lead or be in the limelight.

"What do you want to do?"

"I'm happy by your side," she said with a slight hesitation. I wasn't sure if she was being honest, and felt she wasn't telling me everything.

More wolves approached us, but none touched Carmen. I didn't think my Beast could handle any more of others touching her. Although it wasn't a full moon, some wolves shifted and hunted, which sparked another thought. I hadn't seen Carmen's wolf. She turned to me, understanding my expression, and undressed. She'd seen my wolf, a mix of white and light brown—almost sandy color.

As I removed my shirt Carmen was already naked and shifted into a large dark beast. The power radiating off her in waves made me stop and stare. Her black wolf could easily overshadow some of my strongest. She was a gigantic beast for a female, the color of midnight. When she turned to me, she whispered in my mind to hurry. But all I could do was gape at her, completely dumbstruck, and forgot my previous thoughts.

"You are magnificent, Carmen," I said, scratching

behind her ear. "I'm glad to have you as my mate," I whispered, then shifted.

Carmen was only slightly smaller than me as I stared down at her in my furry shape. We felt each other's joy in that moment and before I thought anything else; she bolted away. I needed to catch her. And catch her I would.

I followed her alongside the stream surrounding our land, running as far as we could. When she finally slowed down and I stood beside her. She'd found a deer.

'Hunt?' she whispered.

'Be my guest.'

I was a stealthy hunter, Jason was too, but Carmen was something else entirely. I didn't see her move. Her dark coat helped her blend in with the shadows as she neared the unsuspecting animal, and I wondered if she could mask her scent. Being so close should've alerted the animal to her presence, but didn't. The deer didn't move. One moment Carmen was off to the side, I knew this because the darkness moved, then she darted to the other side. I sensed her approach, then she leapt on the deer and killed it swiftly and quietly. Once again it left me with a muzzle full of sharp teeth.

I came out of my reverie when Carmen licked my face. The scent of fresh copper left me famished. It was then I realized we had things to discuss. Things we might have omitted, or rather Carmen didn't say. I wouldn't be angry with her, but I was curious as to *all* her abilities even though she had said she had none.

We feasted on the animal until there was nothing left. Normally we'd share such a treat with the rest of the pack, but I wanted to only share it with her.

We took our time heading back to the clubhouse and when we did the sun painted bright colors across the sky. All the others were back, some playing outside in their wolf's form while others were already asleep.

I brought Carmen to my room, and we shifted. Her change back into human form was effortless. I sensed Carmen was more powerful than I'd previously thought. As she shifted her energy pulsed throughout the room making my heart beat faster. I shifted and stood before her with an overwhelming need to kneel before her. I didn't know what to make of it and felt myself step backward. My motion caught her eye and the lines between her eyes deepened.

"What's going on?"

"I don't know. You tell me?"

"I don't know what you're going on about."

"What are you really? And please don't lie. I just felt a burst of your power trying to command me to kneel before you." I folded my arms and stared at her. We were still naked, but sex was not on my mind, although it should be.

Sadness filled the air and tugged on my heart. There was something she wasn't telling me. She sensed my reservations and sat on my bed, shoulders slumped.

"I didn't know what was happening when it first happened," she said.

Her voice tiny and fragile, making me want to run to her and protect her. But I needed to understand what she was first to protect myself and my pack.

"When wolves die, their spirit wolf goes to the spirit world, to the metaphysical realm," she said, and I nodded. When all wolves died, our spirits joined the rest of the wolves. "That's why my parents left me in Krystal Creek. When one of the powerful alphas died back home, I had somehow absorbed his power instead of it going on with him. It strengthened me. My parents didn't know what to do about it. But our leader was unhappy and wanted me

76

gone. At first I thought we were all staying in Krystal Creek, but they left me. John took me in and promised to keep an eye on me until I matured. We hardly had any deaths in our pack, so I didn't think of it again. But when John died, it happened again—I absorbed either his power or his wolf making me..." she raised her arms in defeat. "I am stronger than I was before. Much stronger. And I've been thinking that's the reason it's taken me so long to find a mate. It was probably the fact that males sensed this part of me, but not understanding what it meant. All they knew was they didn't want me. But with you it's different." She glanced at me with unshed tears and my heart broke. I wanted to keep her safe from harm.

I understood it wasn't her fault, and she did nothing wrong. But I was alpha and wouldn't bend knee for another.

"I won't fight you, Carmen—"

"What? No, I don't want that." She shook her head, and a tear slid down her cheek.

"But you understand you have alpha power in you and command that I bend the knee. I won't do it. I can't have that. We have bonded and you're my mate. That will never change. But you need to understand, you and your wolf, we won't be *your* second."

She stood and approached, reached for me and I grabbed her hands, bringing her closer. "I've already said I don't want any of that. I only want to be yours."

"Tell your wolf that," I said, arching an eyebrow. A surge of power thrusted outward and Beast pushed to the surface, sniffing. "Your wolf is out—"

"She wants your wolf. She will obey."

I nodded and kissed her forehead. Her power no longer pushing against me, instead enveloping me in comfort.

Which was her way of showing obedience, her submission, and I appreciated that.

"Did we make a mistake?" She asked quietly.

"About what?"

"About bonding so soon. We should've spoken about this beforehand. I wanted to, but…"

I was quiet for a moment. Thinking. Unsure what to say that wouldn't cause heartache. Were our actions done in haste, in lust, and possibly our demise. I wasn't sure and didn't want to answer her.

"I don't know." Was all I could say. I was completely out of my element. But we'd get through this—we had to. I'd never heard of another wolf absorbing the power of those fallen, but there was so much one never fully understood about the metaphysical realm. But I was glad she was mine and on our side. That meant something.

"A lot has happened and I think we need to rest," I said, cupping her face and planting a soft, delicate, chaste kiss on her lips. We needed rest before we met with the rogue wolves tomorrow, and although Nick had said he would fight them, I couldn't help but wonder if he should. If he died, would Carmen absorb his power too since it happened in close proximity or if it only happened to wolves in her pack. There's much I didn't understand.

She said nothing, only to snuggle herself as close to me as possible.

As Carmen slept in my arms, all I thought was what would happen if I had to fight.

Chapter Thirteen

CARMEN

Although I slept comfortably, something kept me from sleeping deeply. Perhaps it was the fact Shawn may fight the rogue wolves, or I intimidated him by what I could do, even though it was something out of my control. I never asked for any of it.

Or simply Shawn hardly slept himself. I felt his concern not only for the rogue pack, but for my ability and the potential threat I posed to him and his pack.

There was one alarming fact that skittered across my thoughts—Shawn may not have bonded with me if he'd known this beforehand. There was an underlining risk: I might want more power. And where there was more power, there was more risk.

I'd never forget his expression after I'd told him about absorbing other's power. It scared him. Then as if he had read my thought quickly schooled his features. But I'd already seen it. He no longer looked at me with adoration after that.

He stirred beside me, pulling his hand out from mine. I

wanted to reach for him and ask those questions. But something told me not to.

He threw the covers off with a deep sigh and stomped toward the bathroom, closing the door. When I heard a click, I bolted upright and stared at the door. He'd locked it. He didn't want me near him.

Regret crossed my thoughts, and my eyes stung. I swallowed hard and the back of my throat ached.

Shawn regretting our bond shattered my heart into splinters. It physically pained.

We had bonded too soon. We didn't think it through without getting to know one another better.

It was a mistake.

The more I thought about it, the more I realized I was correct. This was wrong. I shouldn't have gone to the retreat. We shouldn't have leapt into a bond without discussing everything first. But I tried to tell him. I did, but whether it was enough I wouldn't know.

An overwhelming thought crossed my mind. He suspected I kept this part of myself from him on purpose, and that I would keep more important information from him in the future.

Then I realized, similarly with contracts, there was an escape clause. The same with bonding. But to sever the tie that bound us, no matter how it would hurt, was possible if done by certain people. It would be a risk and one of us could be hurt, or even die. But I had to try.

In my pack we had a healer of spirits; a shaman. He could help me. I would ask him to cut my ties to Shawn, to set him free. I'm sure he'd rather be alone than with someone who *might* kill him one day. Someone who *might* take over his pack.

Even if it harmed me. I would never hurt him, ever, but would he believe me?

I knocked on the bathroom door.

He responded with a grunt.

"Is everything okay in there?" I stammered. "I feel—"

"It's fine. Just give me a second." His tone was cold and harsh. It felt as though a blade slithered down my spine.

"I'm sorry," I whispered, but knew he heard. "This was a mistake, wasn't it?" I said while dressing.

Shawn made a strange sound I couldn't discern.

"I'll fix this. I'll make it right. We can break the bond and you don't have to fight. Nick could do it. I'd rather set you free than keep you caged, Shawn. My feelings for you run deeply..." I choked, unable to finish my sentence instead I grabbed my bag and left the room.

When I'd left, Shawn hadn't bothered to stop me. He stayed in his bathroom. From his actions, I knew it was the right thing. It was hard for him to face it, to face me.

The cab company I'd called had a vehicle nearby, that by the time I exited the building, it was standing outside waiting for me. I climbed in and gave the address.

Chapter Fourteen

SHAWN

I couldn't sleep.

I felt Carmen beside me the entire time; I felt her heat, the beat of her heart, and sensed her trepidation.

So many foreign thoughts swarmed my mind I couldn't think clearly. But what stood out was clear—we bonded too quickly.

'No,' growled Beast. *'It wasn't.'*

'I know those thoughts aren't right. Bonding with her was the right thing to do,' I said and felt Beast relax.

We wanted her on so many levels. And we were meant for each other. But… the issue of her absorbing the power of those who had lost their lives came to the forefront.

Carmen was powerful, and I only felt it after we bonded; she had hid it from me until it was too late.

'She's ours,' Beast moaned inside my head. I felt him rumble through my chest. He didn't appreciate the thoughts we were having. They weren't our thoughts. They were Carmen's thoughts… maybe?

I needed to stop touching her, to think clearly. I left her

alone in the bed and entered the bathroom. The window was open and the cool air caressed my naked flesh. I closed the door and sat on a folded towel on the edge of the bath. The quarter moon smiled lopsided with sprinkles of stars and soft clouds passed by.

Now that I wasn't so close to her, I breathed deeply.

'She's still ours,' Beast confirmed. *'Don't mess this up!'*

'Yeah, yeah! I'm not trying to mess anything up.' I rubbed my face.

Carmen said something about going somewhere. Her voice barely audible then I heard scraping on the floor followed by keys jangling.

"No, wait. Don't go!" I yelled and opened the door; I tried opening the door. With the door stuck, I pounded harder, yelling at her to wait, but she didn't respond. A cold shiver ran down my spine and my pulse thundered in my ears.

Instead of hearing her response, all I heard were her footsteps as she walked away. She was leaving us.

"No!" I pounded so hard on the door wood creaked. "Carmen!" I yelled through a deep growl. We were being kept apart.

Rage filled me within knowing we were being kept apart on purpose, by whom I did not know. But the moment I got hold of them, I'd gladly sink my fangs into them. With all my strength, I slammed my body through the door, landing with a loud thump on the ground.

Slowly, I climbed to my feet and sprinted down the stairs and out the front door. The cab she'd climbed into had already gone.

Sweat dripped down my spine as if a blade sliced through me. My chest ached. My stomach swirled. I closed my eyes and whispered my thoughts.

'Carmen, where are you going?'

Silence.

'Carmen!'

'I'm going to make it right.' Carmen finally answered.

'Come back. We need to talk about this.'

Silence.

Either she didn't hear me or ignored me. I didn't like either option.

I spun around, grabbed clothing and Nick's keys, then bolted for his car.

Chapter Fifteen

CARMEN

Our building was busy with pack members doing their usual morning chores or families getting kids to school. Some children still attended school with humans, while others home-schooled.

I greeted many as I traversed through the hallway with only one thing on my mind—I needed Trevor. I knocked on his door and before he answered I opened it. He always left his door unlocked, he had said we were always welcome. And he always expected us.

Trevor sat in the lotus position on a carpet facing the window. Vanilla incense wafted in the air with a bell chiming every few seconds.

"No," he said without turning around.

"You don't know what I'm asking you to do."

"I know why you're here, Carmen. And no. I will not sever the bond. You've just found your mate." It was then that he stood up with grace and faced me. Trevor was six feet tall, lean, with flowing white hair. From the back, he looked female until you saw the front and realized he was very male.

His yellow/green eyes sparkled with humor and reached for my hands. "Don't make hasty decisions, honey."

"Please, if you know why I'm here, you'll know what would happen if I didn't go through with it."

"I know and my answer is still '*no*', with a capital '*N*'."

I pushed away from him and felt like a child chastised by her father.

"I've told you before that our ancestors have chosen you to receive their gifts. In over a hundred years they had no-one. Until you came along. I don't know why there's a problem. Because you think your mate would think you're in competition for his higher position?"

I stared daggers into his pretty eyes; their color was unique, and it changed either more yellow or green depending on his mood. Right now they were a fierce green —bordering on his mood changing and warning me to tread carefully.

Exhaling a shaky breath, I folded my arms. "We may have bonded in haste—"

"No, you didn't," he said, standing closer.

"He regrets bonding with me. I tried to tell him everything beforehand. But I didn't think it mattered whether I told him before or after."

"Oh, but it does matter, doesn't it? He has tasted your power and those from our pack. He is a good alpha, Carmen. Give him a chance. Ignore those awful thoughts. They aren't yours." He arched a sandy-brown eyebrow. When he smiled it highlighted his already sharp cheekbones and although his features were slightly on the feminine side, his chiseled jaw made you think otherwise.

"Carmen," he started. "That rogue pack will be here

soon. When they get here, your mate won't be. If I were you, I'd ask him to get here now and stop this silliness."

"Sever the bond, Trevor, please."

"Today is a good day to die, isn't it?"

"What?"

"If I do as you request, both of you will die. They will absorb the pack and the rogues will take the younger females. Do you want that to happen?"

It was a rhetorical question because nobody wanted that to happen. I leaned against the windowsill; the sun heating my back, and a shiver ran through me. I spun around when a car door slammed. Three black SUVs parked outside the entrance, then large men wearing black climbed out. The rogue pack.

"Shit, they're here."

"See…" he grinned. "Aren't you glad I did nothing?"

We were in serious trouble. Yet he was grinning. Sometimes I didn't understand our healer. He would tell us one thing, we'd do the opposite, and he'd grin as if to say he'd known the outcome all along. It's probably the reason he didn't tell us everything he *saw*. Saying he was strange was an understatement.

"If I survive today, you must do it," I said in a firm tone.

Trevor shook his head 'no' slipped on a cardigan and stepped into flip-flops. He exited his apartment behind me.

Shouting erupted downstairs, people running upstairs, and Gina ran down the hallway with Nick behind her.

"Oh, I'm so glad you're here. You won't believe the evening I had." Gina glanced lovingly at Nick, then back at me with a seductive smile.

"I'm happy everything worked out," I said, squeezing her hand.

"Where's Shawn?" she asked with concern etched on her face, slipping her arm through mine

"I think it was a mistake…"

"No, don't say that." She shook her head. "It wasn't. It was good, Carmen. Don't doubt yourself. And trust in Shawn. Whatever it is, you will work it out. And right now Nick is going to save us," she grinned, removed her arm from mine and slipped her hand into her mate's larger hand and descended the stairs.

I was happy for them and relieved Nick was here to help us. I doubted Shawn would come here without me telling him the rogue pack was here and hoped Nick could defeat JT.

I followed close behind the couple and entered the hall where the rogue men wearing black stood like the scariest soldiers I'd ever seen. The first time they'd come and fought John, they weren't as frightening. Now, some were armed with weapons. I couldn't understand why they had armed themselves. We rarely used weapons.

"Let me guess," said JT, the rogue leader. "He's going to fight me?" He pointed at Nick.

If I had to imagine what a serial killer looked like, I'd picture someone like JT. He shaved his hair close to his head, his brown eyes so dark they looked black—reminding me of soulless eyes or the devil. And he had a thick scar that ran from behind his right ear along his jawline and then up to his mouth; similar to a Glasgow smile, but only on one side of his face.

JT was powerfully built with corded muscles and scarred hands, no doubt from all the fist fights he'd been involved in that, no matter how many times he shifted, he couldn't heal those scars.

Not only was JT a scary wolf, but quick and nimble.

He had caught our alpha off guard and in two steps he killed him. It was so fast we barely registered what had happened until we saw John's lifeless body slumped on the ground and JT holding his severed head by his hair. The younger females ran screaming and JT howled with laughter.

It was the most unpleasant fight I'd ever witnessed, and I'd seen a few.

An uneasiness settled in my chest. Things were going wrong so quickly and I didn't know how to fix it. Perhaps if I tried reaching out to Shawn, he'd hear my call. But all I got in response was static noise.

Trevor stood beside me as we watched.

All the wolves from our pack had joined us, all silently praying Nick would win.

The rogue pack filed in and closed the doors to our hall. They pushed tables and chairs to the sides, leaving the middle open for the fight.

"Wait, don't close the doors," I said, reaching out to the rogue who twisted metal around the door handles to prevent them from opening.

The rogue snarled at me. "Touch me again and I'll eat your arm."

I yanked my hand back. Shouting behind me caught my attention, and I faced the action. Nick was a big guy, the largest I'd ever seen. His muscles corded and powerful. The room vibrated with his energy, causing all the hairs on my body to stand on end.

Gina rubbed her arms beside me, glanced my way with unshed tears. Without having to say anything I knew she was worried, she'd only met her mate and the possibility of losing him was there. Luckily, they hadn't bonded yet. If he died, he wouldn't take her with him, but I knew her, she would relapse. She would spiral from grief of losing him. I needed to be strong for her.

None of us want to be part of this rogue pack, especially not the younger females. I glanced to my right, and the girls huddled in one corner, their eyes wide and filled with fear.

JT stormed Nick who blocked the first punch. Nick followed up with a kick to JT's side. When he doubled over, Nick slammed his fist into JT's jaw. JT stood slowly and wiped blood from his mouth.

"Tsk, tsk, tsk. You fight dirty, old man," JT said in an ominous tone that made me shiver. His dark eyes flashed silver, then back to black. His eyes flitted from Nick to me. I couldn't understand why JT gave me any attention, he didn't the last time.

Whatever JT had planned would not end well for us. And I suspected Nick would take the brunt of it. I couldn't allow Nick to fall for us, or have Gina fall as collateral damage.

Shawn hadn't known what time the rogue pack would get here and I couldn't reach him. In that moment I knew I had to do something to protect them Nick and Gina, and our pack.

On instinct, I moved to stop the fight. JT saw me and shook his head slowly. He closed his eyes. Someone whispered behind me. I glanced over my shoulder, but there was nothing. When I turned to witness the fight, no-one moved. JT stared at me and his eyes flashed silver again, reminding me of a machine. It was unnerving.

I continued forward even though JT had warned me.

"Stop!" I yelled as I approached the men.

"What are you doing? Get back," Nick growled, stopping me with a meaty paw on my shoulder.

It was the distraction JT needed. He kicked Nick in the chest, sending him flying across the floor.

"Now it's just you and me," JT said in a sinister tone. He beckoned me closer with a finger and an evil smirk.

I'd sparred with powerful men before and some I'd even won. I was about to slam my fist into JT when Shawn came crashing through the window.

Chapter Sixteen

SHAWN

I didn't like what I saw when I arrived at Carmen's apartment building. Seeing the black SUVs made me shudder. I wondered how many men were here that I'd have to kill. I didn't know this rogue pack, but I was about to meet them.

They had locked the hall doors. I saw no other room large enough to accommodate everyone. Now all I needed was to find a different way inside.

I traversed around the apartment building and entered through a small unlocked gate. The play area was now deserted, and movement inside caught my eye. Nick stood in front of a man wearing black. They were about to fight.

I surveyed the building and saw open windows at the top. I scaled the walls and stopped near the open windows. Nick flew across the room. Carmen approached the rogue wolf and was about to fight him. I couldn't allow her to get hurt and needed to intervene.

To get the attention of the rogue, I needed to do something crazy—like falling through the window. I did so with grace and landed on my feet beside Carmen. I winked at her and stood straight. She stared dumbstruck, then her features morphed into an angry frown. I shrugged. I'd never leave her to face this brute on her own.

The rogue wolf was rough around the edges with scars littering his body, and strange tattoos snaking up his arms and from what I could see chest and neck. His hair shaved close to his head and body bulky but all muscle.

"Hmm, I don't think we've had the pleasure," he purred when he saw me. "You're much prettier than the oaf." He jerked his chin in Nick's direction. "Although I must point out I can only fight one of you."

"I'm fighting him, Shawn——" Nick said, but his tone told me they had hurt him, badly.

"Ah," the rogue said, sniffing the air. His eyes flashed silver, then he added. "You're the alpha leader in Sterling Meadow. Hmm, this could be interesting." The bastard grinned. "And you two are mates." He pointed at Carmen, then me.

The shift in his eyes bothered me, alerting me that he was more than just a wolf. My arms pebbled. Energy from the rogue filled the room, and I stepped backward, reached for Carmen and pulled her in behind me.

I heard Nick behind us. But dared not take my eyes off the rogue. His eyes flashed silver again and foreign thoughts flashed through my mind; Carmen falling to the floor and blood pooling around her. I glanced over my shoulder for a split second and saw her shaking her head. Warning me.

"That won't happen," Carmen whispered, having seen the same vision.

My brows furrowed as I turned toward the rogue again. "You're the one." The rogue smiled, curling his lips over his teeth. It was a combination of a snarl and smile and creepy as fuck. He was the one who had somehow given us those foreign thoughts to drive us apart. He had almost gotten it right. I almost lost Carmen. I squeezed her thigh as I kept her behind me.

"I couldn't have a power-couple stop me, now could I." The rogue leapt in the air and punched me in the throat. He was so quick I hadn't seen him move until I flew across the floor and into the glass door.

"No!" Carmen yelled, slamming her fist into the rogue. The impact snapped his head backward but didn't deter him, it enraged him.

The rogue roared and punched Carmen in the face. I felt her pain as she crashed to the floor.

My blood heated watching her hurt. I flew up in one swift motion, the power of Carmen's pack filled me from within and I struck the rogue with their collective force. Crunching sounded, followed by the rogue crumpling to the ground. I doubted he'd go down and stay down when he grabbed my ankle. I turned and kneed him in the face. Blood sprayed everywhere. His eyes flashed silver and a loud high-pitched sound filled the air, deafening me.

Everybody crouched, holding their ears.

I paused.

The rogue stood slowly. He smashed his fist into my side; I doubled over then returned with an uppercut to his face. His jaw barely had time to heal from the first hit when it snapped loose. He hit again, but I blocked it and kicked his side.

Although the rogue had *other* power, I was a skilled fighter. We each had our strengths. Where the rogue got one punch, I hit twice and harder. But when he smashed his palm into my nose, I saw stars and darkness. He hit again, snapping my head to the side and pain laced down my spine; still able to move my toes. Thankfully, my back only ached and wasn't broken.

Carmen roared and jumped onto the rogue's back. Her power swirled around me. She was angry and hurt. A scary combination for a woman, especially mine.

I grinned. I knew what was coming as her energy pulsed through me.

Carmen snarled, gripped the rogue's throat and tore it out. Blood sprayed everywhere. The rogue fell to his knees then collapsed on his face with Carmen riding his back.

But Carmen wasn't stopping. The rogue twisted, moving onto his back. She stuck her fingers into his eyes and removed the silver orbs. The rogue screamed. A powerful blast rocked everyone back except Carmen. She wouldn't stop until she had his heart. I didn't need her to tell me what she wanted to do, I felt it.

I didn't want her to kill someone so viciously, it would scar her forever. Although it wouldn't be the first time as visions of Nashville came to the front.

"Carmen, no!" I pulled her off the rogue. "Don't or you'll have nightmares for the rest of your life."

"I need to end this," she said, pushing me out of the way. Carmen smacked the rogue's hands away and dug her fingernails into his abdomen, reaching deep inside his ribs and ripped out his heart. She pointed the still beating heart at the rogues in black. "Who's next?" She yelled, ensuring each heard her words. But the rogues raised their hands, surrendering now that their leader was dead.

She bit into the heart, then spat it out. "He was more than just a wolf. Someone made him more powerful. He tastes synthetic, but the magic's gone. He is no more." She dropped the heart and picked up a fallen chair and stood on top of it. "Nobody may tear my pack apart. If it means I lead, then so be it." Her voice echoed in the hall, nobody rising to challenge her.

She glanced in my direction and whispered. "I've been denying my destiny for too long, and now I realize who I truly am. I belong here with them and need to embrace my position. I can't run away from my myself. And I don't want your pack, only mine. We can work it out, I know we can. What I'm saying is, Shawn, I'm yours if you still want me."

I stared, dumbstruck. Carmen was powerful, and flesh hungry. She fought the rogue and killed him, even tasted his heart to figure out what he was. It scared me. She scared me. But Beast still wanted her.

Could I love her knowing what she could do, I didn't know.

Chapter Seventeen

CARMEN

I'd been hiding behind finding a mate instead of standing up for myself and taking what I wanted; my pack *and* my mate. I knew I could do both, I just needed to believe in myself and have the right support.

But I didn't think Shawn wanted me. I doubted I'd ever forget the look on Shawn's face; shock, horror, and possibly regret. He'd seen what I could do without batting an eyelid. I did it on instinct and felt no remorse. And I'd do it again. If it saved my pack, I'd do it.

Gina was happy that I'd saved our pack, and everybody came to congratulate me with hugs and kisses. There were tears and laughter. It relieved some that I'd offered myself as alpha of the pack. They would've accepted a new alpha, but they would've preferred me.

When a cool hand snaked its way around my waist, I knew it was Trevor. "Now aren't you glad I didn't sever the bond," he whispered so softly I barely heard him. "Now go work things out with your mate." He kissed me on the cheek and pushed me toward Shawn.

Nick and Shawn stood against the wall. Both wore grim expressions. Nick started healing, while Shawn only had a few scratch marks.

I approached them. Nick pushed away from the wall, giving me a wide berth. I stood in front of Shawn. His emotions were all over the place; happiness, sadness, even suspicion.

I narrowed my eyes at him but said nothing. My heart pounded in my chest. The thought of losing him greater than before. But the same thoughts still lingered; he wasn't happy.

The muscles along his jaw ticked. His blue eyes darkened and his mouth was in a straight line.

After five minutes of staring at each other, I finally broke the silence. "What do you want?" It was a simple question, yet it held so many answers with hidden messages. Did I want to know what he wanted? I wasn't sure, but we needed to sort things out now.

"You," he said, followed by a low rumbling from his chest. He held out his hand, I slipped my smaller hand inside his and he pulled me alongside him and outside.

We walked in silence. My heart raced. A cold sweat broke out along my skin and I hadn't even perspired when I fought JT. That's how much Shawn affected me. I didn't want to lose him, yet even though he had said he wanted me, his actions spoke louder, and I was still afraid.

Shawn stopped at the border wall where the park ended, and the forest began. He leaned against the wall and pulled me closer. He lifted my arms and placed them around his neck while he snaked his arms around my waist, holding me in place.

"You've scared the living shit out of me not only in that

hall but when you ran away," he said, his tone cold and hard. My chest ached. I felt awful for doing that. He didn't wait for me to reply as he continued speaking. "I now know our thoughts weren't our own. It was that rogue who knew about our bonding and tried to tear us apart. He wanted us to fight, and I knew you came back here to ask your healer to sever the bond. Trevor told me everything. And if Trevor did what you asked, it would've weakened us and the rogue would've won."

I gasped and glanced up, but he shushed me.

"We've waited too long to find each other. And what we've gone through will test us for years to come. I know you won't go after my pack as I won't go for yours. You are now the alpha here, and Sterling Meadow is only thirty minutes away. We can spend alternate nights in the various towns. I will do whatever it takes to ensure we stay together."

I smiled and couldn't stop the tears from flowing.

"Shh," he kissed my temple and wiped away the tears with his thumbs. "Do you still want Trevor to sever the bond?"

I shook my head and mumbled a soft 'no'.

"Good." He gripped my chin and lifted my face. "Don't ever do that to me again. Don't run away, come and talk to me." His penetrating gaze filled with love and longing and I did what any woman would. I rocked onto my toes and kissed him. Shawn held me firmly in place and I never felt his hesitation. He broke the kiss and said near my lips. "You're my woman. Don't ever forget that," he smiled and kissed me chastely.

His hands roamed over my hips and his touch like molten lava burning my skin. My arousal felt like a shot to my core. Shawn pushed me through the opening in the wall and against it on the other side. His pupils dilated and I knew what he wanted because I wanted it, too.

We removed our clothing without destroying them. Our bodies melded and limbs entwined. I couldn't get enough of his warmth surrounding me; I wanted more, I wanted all of him.

We had the forest floor beneath us, the trees above us, and the sounds of the animals and insects music to our ears.

Shawn hovered above me, his eyes flitted closed as he entered my heated sheath. A gasp tore from my mouth as I felt every inch of him. His touch was delicate, and I didn't want him to stop. I'd be happy for us to remain here; just the two of us, alone, naked, and forever.

My body was his in that moment, and he offered his to me. Not only our desire for each other, but we shared our hearts and our souls.

His kisses were delicate against my heating skin as he found his delicious rhythm. Each stroke releasing pent up frustration from the chaotic day.

When Shawn grazed his sharp teeth against my hard nipple, it sent a pleasurable ripple straight to my core and tore sounds from my mouth.

He continued rocking into me with care, moving within me, watching me, loving me. He showered me with kisses as he continued his pleasurable wrath on my body.

The start of a strenuous day ending in ecstasy.

My hands roamed all over his body; as he thrusted deep within me, I reached for his ass and pulled him closer, needing him deeper. As his movements became uncontrolled, I clutched his shoulders and met his powerful thrusts with my own.

The intensity so severe I pressed my mouth to his shoulder and bit down. The taste of his blood swirled around me. He grunted in an animal-like fervor and bit into my shoulder as he released his heated seed within me. I clenched around him, milking him, and the sensation brought on another wave of pleasure.

He stilled but didn't move away. He unlatched his teeth from my skin and I shuddered. I licked his wounds as he licked mine.

As we held onto each other, we communicated with an unspoken language; one that united us and would keep us together forever. And I embraced him.

Chapter Eighteen

SHAWN

I sat behind my desk going over various documents for the pack and the business I had on the side. The door to my bathroom was fixed but I was still waiting for my insurance to pay my claim for the truck; it was a complete write-off.

Noise sounded outside and Carmen burst through my door. At first I was angry, mad even because I didn't sense her arrival. She had told me she would remain in Krystal Creek for the day and I'd meet her there tonight.

I leapt to my feet, to close the distance between us, when she bolted into my arms. She was crying, but with a smile on her face. It completely confused me.

"What's wrong? Why are you here? Did something happen?"

"Jeez, so many questions. Can't a lady see her man?" She said seductively, fingering the hem of my shirt and her fingers walked up my abdomen that sent signals straight to my groin. "Ooh, so happy to see me," she purred, cupping my erection.

"Christ, woman. You're going to kill me." The entire

week Carmen and I had made love like teenagers. I had stamina, but never acted the way I did with her. Ever. This woman drove me crazy and I couldn't get enough of her. I never wanted to stop touching her.

Beast growled within me, and Carmen placed her hand against my chest and kissed me through my clothing.

"Darling…"

I opened my eyes when she didn't finish her sentence. "What? Something wrong?"

"Just the opposite." She reached for something behind her and presented it to me.

I shrieked like a girl when I saw the positive pregnancy test.

"We're pregnant?"

"We're pregnant," she said with unshed tears.

This was a dream come true. We had doubts whether Carmen could fall pregnant. Usually… wolves found their mates early in life and when they bonded and had pups, the female was in her twenties or thirties at the latest.

Carmen was in her forties, never pregnant before, until she met her mate… *me*. I told her we could try, but we didn't have to and we shouldn't push ourselves. The last thing we needed was the additional stress. I guessed, with our late night romps and her… appetite for me… we had somehow created a little pup of our own.

"Oh, honey. You've made my day." I kissed Carmen chastely all over her face and squashed her against me. "This is the best news ever."

She glanced up at me with those bright green eyes, and my heart swelled with love for this woman.

'Our woman!' Groaned Beast.

'Our woman.' I agreed.

Next in the Shifter Days, Vampire Nights, & Demons in between Series

www.vinci-books.com/night

Some monsters don't need fangs to destroy you.

I never took vacations as a vampire. But my sanctuary in South Africa shattered when she walked into my world, awakening something I thought had died long ago. Now, as demon-marked bodies pile up around us, I'm forced to choose: protect the one soul who makes me feel alive again, or surrender to the darkness that made me.

Turn the page for a free preview…

Night Hunter: Chapter One

DECLAN

Watson shuffled into the room, interrupting my meal. I narrowed my eyes at his feet, hoping they'd get chopped off. His shuffling was annoying. Luckily, he only did it on airplanes; it had something to do with balance. I couldn't remember, I wasn't listening when he told me.

I let go of my meal and offered Watson my attention when he cleared his throat at the foot of my bed.

"What is it, Watson?"

He growled, furrowing his brows. "Winston."

"What?"

"My name is Winston, Master. After all these centuries, surely your memory hasn't started to fade."

I arched an eyebrow at the jab and Watson bowed low; almost over doing it.

"Forgive me, Master."

"All right. Now what do you want… Winston." I drawled.

"The pilot will start our descent in about an hour."

"Good, will you clean up this mess?" I pushed the corpse away from my body and climbed out of bed.

"Yes, Master."

"It's a pity though, she was such a good lay, even showed me a trick or two," I grinned, wiggling my eyebrows.

Winston averted his eyes. He wasn't a prude and had seen me naked too many times to count, yet he never stared at me when I stood in all my splendor.

"Why did you kill her then?"

"I couldn't help myself." I was sure the Council would have a fit, but at this moment I didn't care. "And besides, with my tasting limited, I simply couldn't stop. I desperately needed a full meal. The moment her blood touched the inside of my mouth." I licked my lips and tasted a drop of blood I'd missed. "I couldn't stop until her heart did. I'll be full for at least a day." My smile reached my eyes.

"Very well, Master."

"Thank you, Watson." I sauntered to the bathroom to freshen up for our descent and ignored Winston's sigh and the rolling of his eyes.

Winston was such a good sport. I'd been teasing him for years. Who named their child Winston, anyway? How dreadfully awful. And this was centuries ago. Never mind, he was a wonderful man servant and would never leave me.

I stared at my physique in the mirror; a mirror made without silver. Unfortunately, some still weren't able to see themselves. But I was old and powerful enough to see my reflection, toned body and sculptured cheeks. My blue eyes twinkled even. That girl's blood did wonders for my skin. I should stick to under twenties. But never younger than eighteen—a pervert I was not.

My fangs retracted, leaving me with blunt teeth once more.

I dared not scare the riff-raff at the airport. I chuckled to myself, imagining the chaos I'd cause. Vampires had been living out in the open for years, but humans still feared us. As they should.

I showered, washed my hair and dried my body. Once back in my room, I chose a simple outfit, black pants, black T-shirt, my black coat and boots. I was still in my gothic phase and doubted I'd ever leave it. Black, ever elegant, was my color of choice. Red was my second color, naturally.

I finished in time to hear the crackling of the speakers; my private plane was old but functional.

"This is your captain speaking, buckle up." A man of many words.

Plonking down beside Winston, I did as the captain suggested; I may be immortal, but I still got hurt. I spied how Winston wiped his hands with a wet wipe then stuck it in a little bag for discarding.

"What did you do with her body?"

"I opened the hatch while we were still over the ocean. Sharks will get to her soon enough."

"Good ol' chap." My meal had no family, and nobody would miss her. Unfortunately, in today's world we may be more connected than ever, yet some remained lonely.

We landed with a thump on the tarmac and taxied toward the private jet terminal at Cape Town International Airport. It was my first time visiting South Africa and I couldn't wait to see what it offered. I'd heard many wonderful stories about the Mother City that I had to see it for myself, even it if was only once.

As soon as the plane stopped, the pilot opened the door. I walked ahead of Winston, down the six steps, and came face-to-face with the tallest human I'd ever seen. He stood almost seven feet tall, a shaved head, and a nondescript face. He was as average as they came, apart from his height.

"Welcome, Mr. Kieran," the man said as he reached for my hand. I ignored it. He pulled back his hand and continued speaking. "I'm George, your host. How was your flight?"

"Delightful," I smirked. "Is everything in order for our travels?" I eyed Winston, letting him know they needed to be careful with my luggage. My possessions were priceless and dear to me. I wouldn't bat an eyelash killing someone if they damaged anything.

"Yes, Mr. Kieran." George snapped his fingers for the staff to unload our things while Winston barked orders at them. "They tinted the vehicle as per your request, along with reinforcement. Um," George stuttered and violently paged through a booklet. When he found what he was looking for, finally added. "There was a slight issue with your accommodation—"

"What?" I commanded, and George's cheeks reddened.

"Uhm—"

"Uhm? What is it? Spit it out, boy!"

Before, George's accent was very English—similar to those from England with a slight twist, but the more he stammered, the more his accent changed. My brows furrowed at the unfamiliar accent, yet sounding very much like Dutch.

"Isaac, kry vir my die foon."

"Why do you need to phone someone? What is wrong?" I demanded.

George stared at me with frightened brown eyes, deep lines etched between his brows. "You speak Afrikaans?"

It was my turn to frown at him. "Afrikaans? That sounded like Dutch. Aren't you descendants of the Dutch settlers here in Africa?"

George nodded. "Yes, Mr. Kieran. Afrikaans is a

daughter language of Dutch, with a few adopted words from German and Khoisan languages."

"Most impressive and beautiful, and yes, I understand your language. You were saying?"

"Right, why did I need to phone." He glanced nervously at his papers.

A sly smile crept on my face. I think the poor boy wet himself. A strange odor seemed to emanate from his direction, and I wrinkled my nose.

"They weren't able to secure the material needed for your curtains, but they installed a similar quality used in hotels, and added an extra layer for thickness."

"Right, I will see how I manage. And I'll be troubling you if it doesn't work." I glowered down at George, who swallowed hard.

Once he found his voice he added, "Yes, Mr. Kieran," he croaked, coughing into his fist. "I will see if we can source the material you need."

"Good, boy." I patted the top of his strangely shaped, bald head and headed towards the vehicle. "Come, Watson. I want to see the sights."

Winston nodded and made the attendants hurry to load our luggage in the other vehicle.

Night Hunter: Chapter Two

DECLAN

The thirty-minute drive to the secluded and affluent Clifton suburb in Cape Town was breathtaking. The full moon splashed its silver tendrils all around us, hiding behind that gracious mountain. At four in the morning, African time, the roads were quiet with a crisp chill in the air.

The odd vehicle passed on both directions of the highway—which was on the wrong side of the road. I shook my head, these South Africans confused me. A bus with only one light and a door handle missing passed our vehicle; they were most likely employees heading to work or youngsters coming back from a club or bar.

We passed Observatory on our right with Table Mountain on our left, and the silver moon hiding behind it. Our driver, Keith, took the offramp onto Philip Kgosana Drive where we passed homes, hospitals and shopping centers.

After a bit the streetlights became less and less, the road darkened, then we went downhill. Silver light from the moon splashed across the ocean as we travelled the last stretch toward the house I'd rented for the month. Winston had made all the arrangements, to say I was inquisitive was an understatement.

Our quiet driver parked in the driveway and opened the garage door. Once it opened, he parked inside. Winston opened my door and graciously held his hand out for me to grab so I could step out comfortably.

I glanced around the garage and the size of it impressed me; one could easily fit four SUVs with room to spare.

We followed the driver through a door leading from the garage to the foyer, revealing the lavish mansion where five servants waited.

"Good evening, Mr. Kieran," said the man. His eyes flitted to Winston, who no doubt shook his head. The man kept his hands behind his back, sparing me the need to arch an eyebrow at his proffered hand. "My name is Jeff; I am your butler for the duration of your stay. This is Nancy," — he pointed to the next person, — "she ensures everything remains clean and tidy. She will do your laundry and dry cleaning, and will ensure your accommodations are spotless."

Nancy curtsied, averted her eyes like a good submissive. Her blond hair tied neatly in a bun, no makeup, and a slender figure. Awfully young though, if I had to guess she was about twenty. I already liked her.

When she glanced up at me, I winked. She blushed terribly and quickly stared at the floor.

"This is Ursula," Jeff pointed to the next lady who had curly red hair, braided neatly down her back and out of her face. Her bright green eyes filled with mystery, and although she was slightly on the whole-lot-of-woman side, she was pretty.

Ursula curtsied and stared directly into my eyes. I wondered whether she knew what vampires could do with our stares; all I had to do was say the words and she'd do it.

Winston cleared his throat, and Ursula quickly stared at my shoes.

One side of my mouth curved ever so slightly at her defiance, I liked it. She was older, perhaps thirty, maybe thirty-three. She was taller than Nancy, her chest at least a larger C-cup and all natural. I imagined sinking my teeth into those puppies and felt my pants tighten. There was no doubt Ursula saw my erection as her cheeks glowed, hiding her freckles.

"You've met Keith, your driver. We have another who rotates with Keith, and you'll meet him tomorrow when his shift starts."

There was something about Keith I couldn't quite place. He was quiet, suave—but not too much. I caught him stealing glances at Nancy. Perhaps he fancied her, or she was his girlfriend; I'd have to remedy that during my stay.

"And Simon is your chef. He has a menu planned, but you are welcome to change it."

I side glanced Winston who stepped in front of me.

"Perhaps we could have a brief chat," Winston grabbed Simon by his elbow and led him towards the kitchen.

"Allow me to show you around," Jeff offered.

I gave a curt nod and followed.

The ladies scurried away like mice while I followed Jeff around the very overpriced, but lavish mansion. I watched Jeff as he walked in front of me. He was my height, jet black hair cut short and neatly out of his face and shaved around his ears. His chiseled jaw and aquiline nose suited him; I would've thought he would be ugly with that nose, but it actually made him handsome. He wore his black slacks tight, but his black dress shirt fit nicely around his broad shoulders. He spoke about the owners of the house and their other properties in the area which they rented out while they lived in Canada. They frequented here for a months' vacation once a year.

Jeff first showed me the living area with the large glass doors that opened out to a veranda with enough seating for twenty people and a large, heated pool. The house boasted a home automation system I could program to my liking. I'd get Winston to ensure everything was closed during the day. Jeff showed how the glass doors closed and with the flick of a button the black tinting darkened the rooms—which I liked very much.

Next, we went to the six bedrooms one floor up, each with their own bathroom. They had altered the master bedroom specifically to my needs, which included thick, black curtains. They managed to acquire similar curtains to what I'd specified, which they would switch out the moment they received the ones I really wanted. For the hefty price tag I was paying, I expected nothing less.

There was a cinema, gym, and bar area. They even had a separate twin-bed spa room where Ursula doubled as the masseuse. Unless I preferred the touch of a male, then Jeff would be my go-to-guy.

I winked at him when he said that, and the man blushed salmon. I told him I had no preference, whoever was available would suffice.

"The staff sleep on the premises, in the lower level," Jeff said, pointing at the stairs near the front door that led down.

"Do you think it's fair?" I asked.

"What do you mean?"

"That someone like me, can stay here," — I lifted my arms at all the rooms, — "yet they packed the staff tightly like sardines below. Most likely similar to that on cruise ships."

Jeff blanched, and his American accent slipped. He sounded very South African as he stuttered. "No, absolutely not. It is our job, and we get paid well—"

"How often is this house rented out?"

"It's booked a year in advance."

"But you managed to squeeze us in?" Winston had contacted them two weeks ago to enquire about our stay, and they'd promptly provided us with their availability. Either Jeff was lying and it wasn't booked out for the year, or Winston was just that convincing.

"Yes, well, uh…" His accent reverted to sounding American and his cheeks their healthy shade of pink once more. He kept combing his fingers through his hair and stared nervously at me.

I grabbed the hand before he could run it through his now oily hair, stared into his lovely dark eyes and spoke. "Relax when you're around me, Jeff. Just do everything I ask, never utter a word of my wants and needs, and I'll reward you very kindly," I said in my velvety tone that made women drop their panties. "Nod if you understand."

Jeff licked his lips and nodded. His gaze slightly hazy. I let go of his hand even though his hand lingered, needed to hold on to me. When he finally let go of my fingers, he coughed into that same hand, and blinked a few times as he glanced around. Then when he saw me standing closer, he swallowed.

"Do you want me, sir? Ah… I mean, do you need anything, Mr. Kieran?"

I stifled a chuckle, but I smiled warmly. I enjoyed the company of men and women depending on my mood. Men's bodies were hard and always ready. While women's bodies were soft and delicate and always needing to wait for their flower to open for me. I shivered at the delicious thought.

"Help me with my jacket." I turned my back on Jeff. He stepped closer, and I felt his heat against my chilled body. He grabbed my collar and gently pulled off my jacket, careful not to touch me. Good boy.

"I'll just keep it here." He dashed off to hang it in the closet near the front door. He turned to look my way, his eyes large as saucers. No doubt hoping I hadn't seen the bulge in his pants. I missed nothing.

Winston entered the living area with a glass of sherry, handing it to me. "Would you like to sit by the fireplace this morning, Master?"

I took the glass out of his hand, sniffed the aroma and sipped; sweet, sharp, delectable. I nodded and followed my minion to the next room where the fire blazed.

"Please let us know if you require anything else—"

I flicked my wrist, and the door closed, abruptly ending Jeff's sentence. He was so young with much to learn. I fancied him, and only time would tell what happened during my stay.

"Are there many tourists around?" I asked as I sat in a large leather chair. It was old, but still in mint condition.

"The travel agent said few, and Simon agreed. The houses on either side are holiday rentals too. We may or may not see anybody, or we'll see a rush of beachgoers. We'll see."

I nodded my understanding and had another sip. It did nothing to me, but it helped the mundanes relax around me. It was the right color, rich, maroon, and thick; slightly chilled, although I preferred the real stuff warm and straight out the bottle.

"What time does the sun rise?" I glanced outside. The large moon splashed its silver glow against the water, animating the waves. I saw the private beach below, no doubt I had a private entrance.

"During the winter months, the sun rises just after seven."

I nodded and stared at the wicked flames in the fireplace, angry sparks doing their best to escape. In one swift motion, I stood and floated towards the door and opened it with a flick of my wrist. I stepped out onto the balcony and the sea air greeted me. The sounds of the waves were loud in the quiet night. The stars twinkled brightly, surrounding the moon in all her glory. The sun wouldn't rise for another two hours. Glancing left and right then behind me and Winston nodded—no doubt knowing my thoughts.

I levitated high above the house, ensuring none of the occupants saw me, and slowly started my descent towards the soft sand.

Turning back, the lights in the house dimmed, and I silently thanked my minion for looking after me. I drank the rest of the sherry and threw the empty glass in the ocean; a soft plonk as it struck a wave.

I removed my shoes, socks, pants and coat, followed by my shirt and entered the water. "Christ, it's cold," I mumbled to myself. As old as I was, water this freezing still struck my vampire bones. After a moment, the chill subsided, and I swam farther out.

The waves calmed my frantic mind; I had decisions to make that would change everything, hence my vacation.

After my swim, I picked up my clothing and walked towards the entrance to the house. I raised my head when a sound caught my attention; a lullaby sung by a woman with a sultry voice. I narrowed my eyes at the pathways weaving through the houses near the private beach and caught sight of her sandy brown hair, then her face as she came around the corner. I blended in with the shadows for fear of scaring her with my naked body; I didn't want my conquests frightened so soon, although it would be fun. No, I wanted to watch her. I wanted to see what she was doing at this godly hour.

The young woman glanced around nervously, much like I had done earlier, thumbed her shirt strap, and pulled it down. Her naked breasts spilled free. They were beautiful. She pulled her top down her hips and in one swift motion pulled her shorts down too.

My cock hardened at the thought of ravishing her body. But I wanted to watch her first. So instead of launching myself on her, I continued watching, and most definitely drooling.

She sauntered to the water's edge and froze the moment the cold water touched her right foot. She winced when both feet got wet followed by swear words. She shuddered as she continued walking in, then dived into the water with the next wave.

I pulled on my pants and left the rest of my clothing in a heap and sat myself down beside her clothing. She hadn't noticed me yet. I was sure she'd scream the moment she saw me gawking at her. I could always silence her quickly.

When she finished swimming, she walked slowly out with the waves, heading to her clothing. She combed her fingers through her wet hair, pulling it out of her face and squeezed the water out. The moment her eyes flitted to her clothing, and then to me, she froze.

In a moment like this I waited for the ear-piercing screams that ensured others ran to help her, but she surprised me. She just stared, possibly intrigued by the half-naked, wet man sitting near her clothing.

"A girl swimming naked by herself is a recipe for disaster." I taunted, licking my lips.

"Nobody comes here this time of the morning." She cocked her head to the side as her gaze raked up my body.

"Do you swim every day?"

"I prefer the quiet of the early morning to the busy day."

I loved night owls.

She walked towards me with a seductive smile. "Are you enjoying the show?" she asked as she picked up her shirt and slipped it on.

"Oh definitely, I think this is the best reality TV show I've ever seen."

Her smile reached her eyes as she picked up her shorts and pulled them on. Her breasts wet and shining through her thin top, teasing me. She was not a shy girl.

"I'm over there," I pointed at the mansion behind us.

Her eyes widened, then she quickly schooled her features. "Oh," she said nonchalantly. "I stay up there, with my folks."

"Do they know you come here early in the morning?"

"No," she giggled. "What fun would that be?"

I stood, pretending to struggle even though I didn't. "Declan." I proffered my hand. Usually, I hated touching humans, but this girl was different. I wanted her to touch me.

"Lana," she shook my hand, delicately yet confidently. "You're American?"

"Born and bred, and you're South African?" I reached for her face and pulled strands of hair from her cheek. She closed her eyes and swallowed hard, I smirked and neared.

Her heart raced, her chest heaved, and her hard nipples brushed against my chest through her clothing. I caught the strap of her top between my fingers and near the shell of her ear I said, "So beautiful." I trailed my finger down her collarbone, and between her breasts. Her breath hitched and her eyes shot open. I stood back and admired the trembling puddle before me.

Lana swallowed again, then started biting her bottom lip. "I… uhm," she finally said, glancing over her shoulder. There was only one other light on at a house nearby I guessed was her parent's. "Uh," she continued her stuttering.

Then the little minx caught me off guard by wrapping her arms around me, pressing her wet body against mine and pulling me down to her. The moment our lips touched I didn't hold back, I bruised her mouth with mine, and I swallowed her whimpers. I pulled her closer, one hand at the back of her head to keep her in place and the other between us as I reached between her legs. Her pants were damp against her cold, wet skin. She moaned the moment my fingers trailed between her shorts and went lower. Her mound neatly trimmed and her folds slick with desire.

But I wouldn't do her here, not like this, I wanted the privacy to taste her as I pleasured her body, and having sand caught everywhere was not fun. I slowed the kiss, her tongue tasting mine, and I removed my hand from her delicate folds. She moaned her frustrations as she regained consciousness and what I was not doing. I cupped her face to stop the kiss. But I continued staring into her emerald-colored eyes.

"Are you allowed out the house during the evenings or do you seek permission from your parents?"

"Uh," she licked her lips and cast her eyes back at the

house again. "I actually stay in my parents' guest house until I find a place of my own, so no, I don't need their permission. Anymore." Her cheeks flushed when her eyes flitted to mine once more.

"Come to this house," — I pointed at the rental mansion again, — "tonight at nine."

"Okay," she rocked onto her toes and kissed me chastely. "See ya later." She skipped like a schoolgirl back to the house with the bright light. She opened a side gate and slipped out of sight.

I didn't know what it was about Lana, but she intrigued me. She was young, possibly mid-twenties, with a very naughty streak. And I'd love to taste it.

Once I was back inside my suite, I enjoyed a hot shower. My clothing already packed in the closet and my bathrobe set out on the bed. I dried and pulled my robe against my body, tying it in front.

"Have you eaten Watson?" I asked.

He grunted at my name calling again, but answered, anyway. "Yes, behind the house are woods where wild animals roam; tonight, I had a wild hare."

I arched a dark eyebrow. "Wild hare? Are you even full with that measly snack? God, look at you. You could easily eat a deer without coming up for air." Winston was on the short side, but incredibly strong and built like an ox. When he shaved his hair like now, one hardly noticed it was red, unless he grew a beard—which, thank heavens, he shaved before our trip. And he no longer shuffled now that we were safely on land.

"Yes, well, I'd rather not draw attention to us and certainly not so early in our stay." That was a low jab from him. He obviously saw my interaction with Lana.

"She's coming over tonight at nine, ensure there are

refreshments for our guest. The sun will rise soon, and I'll be dead to the world. As always, nobody may enter here while I sleep."

"Yes, Master. If that's all, then I shall retire myself."

Winston picked up the remote, pressed a button, and the smart glass changed to black, and the thick blinds closed. He then closed the additional black curtains I'd asked them to install, just in case some idiot played with the remote and opened the windows in my room. I was not a day walker and would burn to dust if that enormous ball of fire touched my skin.

I locked the door after Winston left, removed my robe and climbed under the satin sheets, cool and smooth against my naked body. The moment I felt my body weigh down, I knew the sun was rising, and I died.

Night Hunter: Chapter Three

DECLAN

The next evening Keith brought us to Cape Town Waterfront. The road he drove on was scenic along the coast through Sea Point, Green Point and then the Waterfront.

The smell of fish assaulted my nostrils as the wind whipped across the waves, spraying light mist along the seawall. The Waterfront's bright lights felt surreal as more people approached the busy mall.

In the distance was Table Mountain. The atmosphere of just standing here, casting my eyes at the sights, was something I'd never experienced before. It did however remind me of the time I went to Dubai where there's ocean, sand, heat, and modern skyscrapers alight with colors. But the Mother City air was different; the various smells of ocean, food, sweets, and lust filled my nostrils, and I couldn't wait to see what else it had to offer.

Instead of going through the mall and sea of bodies, I headed toward the Clock Tower while Winston tended to some shopping. He was worse than a woman addicted to buying stuff. I rolled my eyes when he just about squealed when he saw the For Sale signs.

I left Winston to do his thing and crossed the V&A Waterfront Swing Bridge, heading toward the Clock Tower and the various shops surrounding it. On the opposite side stood another building for one of the more popular banks with various hidden passages and dark corners. There used to be a Ripley's Believe It or Not shop, but it had closed. In the corner stood a lady-of-the-night, my favorite, while I her hunter-of-the-night.

A security guard watched me intently; arched eyebrow, thick lips in a tight line and dark beady eyes on me. Then I realized his face remained in that state at every passerby. Three children distracted him, threatening to drop ice cream everywhere while their parents tried desperately to get them away from the Lindt chocolate store. I pitied the fool who had children; they were vile and needy creatures. Ick.

A sound caught my attention. I turned to face her, a smile splitting my face in two. With a finger, she beckoned me closer; a keen sense of smell for the money in my pocket. Her dark eyes luring me to her dark web. I obliged and followed her.

I asked for her rate, which was extremely cheap considering the Rand-Dollar exchange rate. I handed over the notes; she gasped, stating it was too much. And before her suspicion overruled her emotions, I pushed her farther into the dark corner and covered her screams with my larger hand. Her caramel-colored skin radiant and enticing. Her scent years at this job, but I didn't want what was between her legs. I wanted what coursed through her veins. The delicious red juice that made my mouth salivate.

"It's going to be fine, my dear. I will not hurt you. I give you my word," I said. My tone velvety smooth as she nodded her understanding and started to relax, no longer needing to scream for help. I removed my hand from her mouth as she continued to stare at me, lost within my dark eyes.

My fangs elongated, my hunger stirred, and I bit into my dinner. I hummed my pleasure as she sank against my body, no longer able to fight against the numbness shooting down every limb. My bite was potent; it never hurt, but it never pleasured either. My bite filled with venom, making my victims numb. If I wasn't careful, I'd kill.

Her sweet blood hot and delicious going down my throat. I wanted more but I'd stop. I pulled away before her heart gave in. I never killed ladies-of-the-night; they had an important job, and they did it well. And I always paid enough. She could go straight home and recover from a bout of the flu for a couple of days.

Carefully, I laid her against the floor of the dark alley and slipped two more notes into the pocket near her breast so her Manager couldn't take his share while she recovered.

I slipped through the alleys, back over the swing bridge and met up with Winston where our driver waited.

Full, happy, and horny; I was ready for my date with Lana.

Night Hunter: Chapter Four

URSULA

The vampire crossed the swing bridge, and I ran after him, ensuring I didn't lose him again among the sea of bodies. He was a zippy American bastard who had caught my attention years ago. I needed to watch him in his natural habitat—in the dark shadows.

After monitoring his actions from afar and for so long, I had to get closer when I heard he was finally coming to my country. I had to keep watch over him while he was here. I'd researched many supernatural's, but Declan was the one who had caught my eye and I needed to know everything about him.

I watched him stalk towards the shadows, focused and unrelenting. An exceptional vampire who made my heart stutter in my chest, and desire bloom in my core. All I wanted was one taste, one night with him, to sate my appetite. To feel his cold, hard body pressed against mine. I shuddered at the yummy thought. If others knew about my desires, they'd think I lost my mind, but I was sane and pursued the night hunter.

Just when I thought I'd lost him, I heard children screaming, ice cream falling and the security guard yelling. But there was something else. The hairs on my forearms stood up, making me shiver.

To my right, I heard it. I narrowed my eyes toward the dark shadows. My heart raced while my breath caught in my chest. If he caught me watching, he would kill me for sure. I needed to play this carefully.

I hid near the now vacant shop and carefully walked along the dark wall.

He moved in the shadows; I caught his coat billowing as he moved. I stepped closer. His hand was over her mouth while his other kept her body up.

My chest rose and fell as I watched. I felt like a mouse caught in his trap.

She lay limp against him, unseeing and unmoving. I wondered what his bite felt like as I reached for my neck, craving his touch. I desperately wanted this. I wanted him. But... what if... then again, my what ifs usually ended badly. The risk of him killing me was great. I liked my life. Well... not really, but it was mine to ruin as I saw fit. And I wanted to do this. I needed to do it.

Slowly he sat her down, fixed the hair he ruffled and added more notes in her secret breast pocket. He was forever the gentleman.

I squeezed between the two brick buildings as he passed. I'd wait a few minutes before heading back to my car then back to work where I'd bump into him again. And I couldn't wait.

The woman on the floor stirred as she slowly awoke, a smile flirted across her face even though it was marked with confusion. She probably knew she encountered a john but wouldn't remember what had happened. She touched the side of her neck where he'd punctured her skin. And I cursed myself for not bringing my camera. I pulled out my cellphone, removed the flash and filmed her recovery.

A blast of wind slapped me in the face, and I almost dropped my phone. The woman shrieked. I corrected my hand to record her again.

A dark figure loomed over her, abruptly picked her up, nestled his face on the other side of her body and bit into her. She cried as she tried to move but was incapable. He shoved his hand down her throat to silence her, breaking her jaw. Her eyes bugged as her arms lay limply at her sides. He pulled her head from her neck, then devoured her insides greedily.

I whimpered and covered my hand over my mouth. Tears streamed down my face. Everything happened so quickly. The thing was swift, dangerous, and in an instant gone. Wind blasted past me again as I steadied my phone. It left behind a mangled mess. Her insides were outside and her head barely on her shoulders. But the bite of the vampire remained visible for authorities to see.

Grab your copy...
www.vinci-books.com/night

About the Author

A Multi-genre author writing twisted endings...

N Gray is a USA Today Bestselling Author who lives in Cape Town, South Africa, with her daughter and adopted cat named Miss Beans.

During the day, she's an analyst and provider profiler for a medical insurance company. At night, she types on her curved keyboard, creating fictional characters some may love and others you want to kill yourself.

She writes in four genres: urban fantasy, thriller, horror, and paranormal romance.

She now writes under Natalie Michaels for her new thrillers and SD Syns for her new horrors.

Acknowledgments

With special thanks to Aizlynne.

To my daughter, who keeps asking me when can she read my books, and I keep telling her when she turns eighteen. Thank you for keeping me on my toes. Mama loves you.

Thank you to my readers, old and new, for taking a chance on my books.

You are the reason I write the stories I do. As long as you keep reading, I'll keep writing.

I'm truly humbled by your support and encouragement.

I write in as many genres as I love reading in. There are so many stories swarming inside my head that I could never just choose one.

Horror is my guilty pleasure. I love writing short stories filled with dark humour and the occult with a twist ending.

Urban fantasy and paranormal romance are where I love to spend my time, and I have so many books planned that I don't have enough time (*but I'll get there*).

And lastly, my thrillers. Who doesn't love sitting on the edge of their seat while reading about what goes on inside the antagonist's mind? Well, I love writing about them.